TAVERN
A HISTORICAL NOVEL
BASED UPON
AN EARLY SAN FRANCISCO SALOON
AND
THE FAMILY
THAT OWNED AND OPERATED IT

Author Reputation Press LLC
45 Dan Road Suite 5
Canton MA 02021
www.authorreputationpress.com
Hotline: 1(888) 821-0229
Fax: 1(508) 545-7580

Ordering Information:
Quantity sales. Special discounts are available on quantity purchases by corporations, associations, and others. For details, contact the publisher at the address above.

Printed in the United States of America.

| ISBN-13: | Softcover | 979-8-88853-380-2 |
| | eBook | 979-8-88853-379-6 |

Library of Congress Control Number: 2023905898

TAVERN

A HISTORICAL NOVEL
BASED UPON
AN EARLY SAN FRANCISCO SALOON
AND

THE FAMILY

THAT OWNED AND OPERATED IT

BRYAN JOHN FARRELL

AuthorReputationPress®
Creativity & Branding

A historical Novel based upon an early San Francisco saloon and the family that owned and operated it.

The two styles of text denote the narrator's story over 28 days and the story's history in 23 chapters.

Table of Contents

Tavern's Owners

Nickelas Wagner 1861

Chris David 1877

Gregory Montgomery 1908

Fredric Jack Wagner 1914

Paul Montgomery 1932

Albertina Montgomery 1932

Richard Goodrich 1937

Johnny Goodrich 1983

Homeward Bound

My Turn at The Tavern

I've noticed lately that I'm pretty much invisible. I understand why, I'm too old to be a rival to the men, too old to be considered a possible lover to the women. So before I completely fade into the abyss. I must tell you this story. It begins with my homeward journey. I had left San Francisco as a boy many years ago. The US Navy had been my home and family for years and I had no intentions of returning to the San Francisco family. I was running away from myself and the family tradition, running a saloon. As it turns out, I could not run away from it either. When my mother departed this world, I was the sole remaining heir and I returned to San Francisco to deal with my inheritance.

Day 1 Thirteen Coins

It was one of those foggy San Francisco summer mornings, the fog horns were blowing, there was condensation dripping from the power lines on Grant St. The front doors were bolted closed. There was a note posted on the door "CLOSED UNTIL FURTHER NOTICE". Although the Tavern had been closed for a while it still had a bar's smell that seemed to be drifting through the narrow crack between the double doors. The varnish on the doors, where not worn off by a hundred or so years of use, was cracked and yellowed. I stared at those doors for quite a while, I thought about the thousands of souls over the years seeking refuge here. I thought about the tales my uncle had told about our family that had operated it over the years.

Even through the dim early daylight, I could see that the interior of the Tavern looked exactly as I remember it, as if it was impervious to time, as if one of the working ladies from the long ago Barbary Coast might emerge from the shadows. God, I thought to myself, this is the last thing in the world I want to do. To return here and continue to run this saloon. No way, I was not going to be another family member to squander years of my life tending bar, being a bouncer, a For Free psychiatrist and all. I was going to sell this place, break free, travel the world, anything but not continue the family tradition.

For the first time in years, I thought about that old leather handbag and the old stuff in it. I was overwhelmed by the desire to check out the contents and I hoped that it was still there.

I remember the first time I saw the old purse, my uncle took it out of the safe in the bar. The leather was stiff, the brass appointments tarnished, and the pearl handled yellow with age. My mother would leave me with her brother, Paul while she went shopping. My uncle would take me with him while he cleaned up the bar. I remember the smell of alcohol, tobacco and people that would greet us as he opened the door, it would become a familiar smell. It was in the morning before the Tavern was opened for business and the night crew as usual had not done a good job of cleaning. My uncle cursed them as he put away empty bottles and washed dirty glasses. Even with all the lights on it seemed dark and old.

There was a painting of an almost nude lady. It was high on the wall with a hundred years worth of dust, smoke and time caked on its surface. My uncle said he'd heard that the woman was his Grandmother, the owner of the Bella Union, a bar and dance hall that had closed long ago. He said that the purse belonged to the bar but I could look inside it but not to take anything. It smelled old, contained some old stuff and a small box.

Now that my mother had passed away, I was the new owner of the Tavern and the custodian of that old stuff. I was quite relieved to find it there, almost as if I'd been the last person to handle it. I sat there in the empty bar examining the contents of the handbag. There was a small box containing thirteen silver coins and as I inspected the coins, turning them in my hands, they seemed to be charged with some unknown force. I did not know it at the time but they were Spanish, hand minted from Mexican silver. And there were things I wished I never knew about the coins. That the silver had been raped from the earth by Aztec slaves, stolen by the Spanish Conquistadors and paid to the Pontiff as ransom for their mortal souls. I was not quite sure if it was just my imagination but as I held them I'd feel the presents of Sarah my Great Great grandmother. And when I read the almost pornographic poem about a sexual encounter between an Ursuline nun and a young girl and held the silver coins I could feel her pain and loss of faith. As I shifted through the other contents in the safe, I found a receipt for passage for three from New Orleans, two small Ivory crosses, a letters, a prom, some medals, an old yellowed newspaper chipping about a killing in Virginia City, the typed letter to me from my uncle written years ago, and a number of handwritten notes by my great grandmother.

Later that night as I sat in the empty bar room turning the thirteen silver coins over and over, a strange warm feeling of being home overcame me. The smell of liquor, tobacco and people accompanied by the late-night city serenade, muffled auto horns, distant sirens and frog horns, so imprinted in my youth caused a rush of memories. Memories of my uncle Paul, my mother and a host of long forgotten friends. A noise near the entrance drew my attention. I instinctively asked "Who's there". A young lady emerged from the shadows and replied "you know who I am". She was young, maybe still a teenager dressed in a yellow dress with white fringe to accentuate the details. She looked as if she just stepped out of a Gone With The Wind movie set. "No, I do not, I do not believe I know you. How did you get in here?" I replied. As she slowly walked towards me, there was something familiar about her. Her friendly smile and kindly eyes displace my fears with curiosity. She again said "you know who I am". This time I recognized a southern accent. I asked her name? she replied "you will have to guess my name" She continued to walk towards me and with extended arms she said " you have always known me" I instinctively raised my hand to resist her invitation. I could see her disappointment as tears began to fill her dark brown eyes. "Please just touch my hands, I am your portal to the past and you must make the journey if you wish to know who you are." With tears in her eyes she said " I must leave now but I can return when you are ready and know my name". "And how will I learn your name?" I asked. "The same way as you found my coins" she said.

"Sarah," I whispered to myself, " Sarah my great something grandmother." No way, I thought to myself. I must be dreaming or having a nightmare. " Sarah," I said out loud. She smiled, a knowing sad smile and said " Yes, I have committed the gravest of sins, disloyalty to this family, and myself. I must atone for my mistake."

everything is temporary,

pain makes it seem permanent

Chapter 1
1854 Lost of Innocence and Faith

New Orleans as many of the world's major cities was built on the edge of a river, the Mississippi. The city's roots go back to the early seventeenth century when the Spanish established a settlement on the high ground at the curve in the river just a few miles Gulf of Mexico. Because of its strategic position on the mighty Mississippi river, New Orleans was coveted by many nations and it had changed hands a few of times before the Montgomery family established their home there. A rigid social hierarchy had developed over the last century. At the apex was the old established Spanish and French Creoles family, next where the financially successful Yankees followed by free blacks and at the bottom the newcomers mostly Irish and Italian emigrants. The African slaves were not socially ranked because they were considered property, valuable property.

Sarah Duplin Montgomery 1840 – 1866

Sarah was the first child of the Montgomery's. She was a bright loving child with a wonderful future . Her mother, Louis Duplin was a second generation native of New Orleans. Her parents had fled France just after the great revolution. They had been aristocrats with large holdings of property. They had backed the Royalist but had decided to flee France for Spain and wait out the turmoil. When it became clear the Royalists had lost, The Duplin moved to New Orleans to join other French expatriates. The Duplin claimed to be a descendent of Charles II through the illegitimate son known as The Bastard of Orleans.

Although the Duplin's fortunes did not fare well in their new country, they maintained a regal air and succeeded in marrying their daughter to the social upcoming Northern family, the Montgomerys.

Sarah's father, James Robert Montgomery, was a first generation of New Orleanians. His parents had moved to New Orleans in the early 1800's. Robert, his father, had started a trading company and had prospered. While the strict class code of New Orleans limited Montgomery's social status, their money gained them respect and influence. For the Duplins, James was a fine suitor for their daughter, Sarah's mother and would add a measure of security to their own prospects.

Sarah was raised to be a good Catholic wife and mother. Her formal education was limited but she was well grounded on domestic skills. She could speak a little French which she had learned from her grandparents, but English was her first language. Her life at their uptown house was grand. She was loved and protected. Sarah was her father's favorite. The family celebrated the Christian holidays, but Christmas and Easter were Sarah's favorite. Her mother would take Sarah shopping in the Vieux Carré, Old Square. Her favorite colors were yellow and white and the Vieux Carré was the best place to find a little girl's dress. As Sarah approached puberty, she blossomed into a beautiful young lady. She had inherited her father's curly light brown hair, dark brown eyes, and bright smile, but not her father's intelligence or independent nature. Rather Sarah tended to be needy and a follower like the mother.

Just before her thirteenth birthday yellow fever struck the household. The yellow fever seemed to come in waves, sweeping over New Orleans in those days every few years. The wave of 1854 was especially devastating; it seemed that almost every other person had been affected. Sarah became quite sick and was bedridden for over a month. She was delirious most of that period and was unaware that her parents and two siblings had succumbed to the disease. Sarah's French aunt and her husband assumed control of her father's business and property.

Being a young female in this period, she had only one option, to live under their paternalism. Sarah had gone from a loving household to one where she was abused and barely tolerated.

Betrayal

Sarah's aunt had little use for her but Henry, her husband, on the other hand had a keen interest in her. It started with looks that Sarah instinctively understood. She tried to become invisible and avoid him. But the looks soon became unwelcome touches and body brushes. Then he started cornering her and exploring her body with his hands. She hated his smell, his rough probing hands. One night his intent came to fruition. He entered her bed reeking of tobacco, alcohol and desire. She cried silently and tolerated his repressive weight as he stole her virginity, her innocence. She hoped that perhaps by enduring his transgression she'd gain more favorable treatment. She understood that she was prostituting herself but felt she had no options. After a few nights of this, she found that she could divorce herself from the physical world and escape mentally to better times - a time with her family, her sister, her grandparents, her mother and father. Her Aunt became suspicious and confronted her. She was happy that it was out in the open and hoped her aunt could provide some shielding from that man. After a few days of heated arguments between the aunt and her husband, it was decided that Sarah would be sent to the Ursula Convent.

Virgin Martyrs

The Order of St. Ursula, the model of consecrated virginity, was dedicated to the education of young women. The patron saint of the convent was St. Ursula. She was the first of the eleven virgins, Ursula, Sencia, Gregoria, Pinnosa, Martha, Saula, Britula, Saturnina, Rabacia, Saturia, and Palladia, of Cologne, the virgin martyrs. St. Ursula, the namesake of the Order was a legendary princess, a daughter of a Christian British king who traveled to Europe in the company of eleven maidens. Ursula and her company were captured by a pagan lord, tortured in an effort to get them to renounce their Christian Faith but they held to their faith even in death.

The Ursula Convent was located across town from the Vieux Carré. Sarah had passed it many times in her trips about town with her parents. As Sarah left the house, the house that had been home, the house with all those wonderful memories of her family, her aunt handed her a large leather handbag, sometimes called a day bag, that had been her grandmother's. She'd so love that bag. It was so beautiful with a brass handle with an inlaid mother of pearl. In the bag were all her worldly possessions.

After the initial interrogation by the Mother Superior, Sarah was given a new name, Martha, as was the custom in the convent, and assigned to a dorm with ten other girls. She was given a loose-fitting gray gown made of coarse material. She was told to dress in the gown and to place her belongings into her leather handbag and that her belongings would be stored; she would no longer require her worldly belongings since she was in God's hands now.

Some of the girls had been in residence for many years, coming to the convent as young orphans. Others were new arrivals, like Martha (Sarah), recently displaced and often from the street. They were considered the lucky ones because the alternative was a life of abuse and early death. Life at the convent was tough with a strict behavior code and harsh duties. Even so, the girls were happy to be somewhere that provided shelter and food. Within a few days of Martha's arrival, one of the girls warned her not to attract Mother Superior's attention.

Martha did not really understand the warning. She did not know what was meant by "attracting her attention". Mother Superior was a woman of God. What harm could it cause? The girl said the other girl that did always disappeared. Martha did her best to adhere to this advice and tried to be invisible and blend in with the group of girls. Mother Superior would have regular inspection of the girl's dorm and of the girls themselves. After inspecting the dorm, Mother Superior would have the girls line up for a physical inspection. She was always careful not to physically touch the girls but she thoroughly inspected them. It seemed to Martha that with each inspection Mother Superior was spending more and more time inspecting her. Sarah began to notice that the other girls treated her differently and no longer looked directly at her. They would never allow their eyes to meet Martha's.

One evening while the girls were readying for bed, Sister Sencia came to the dorm. A hush of fear seemed to fill the air. She came directly to Martha, took her by the hand and without speaking led her to a small room, closed the door and left her there alone. The room had a cold stone floor and no windows. Martha had never been there before; it was cold and dark and absolutely quiet.

What seemed like eternity but was only a few minutes, Mother Superior came in carrying an oil lamp, her habit seemed more starched and tidier than ever. She closed the door behind her, extinguished the lamp and stood directly in front of Martha. After a moment of hesitation, Mother Superior slipped her left hand through the loosely fitting neck of Martha's nightclothes, placed it on her small right breast and slowly began to massage the nipple. Martha tried not to take pleasure in this but could not help herself. Her breathing became heavy. She could hear Mother Superior breathing in short, deep sporadic spurts. She felt Mother Superior's right hand under her nightclothes, between her thighs. She felt Mother Superior hand touch her. Her hands were warm, so soft and knowledgeable.

Martha could feel the aching growing in her groin. As Mother Superior's finger slipped smoothly in and out with an erotic rhythm, she could feel the swelling and then the explosion came. Mother Superior began to tremble, her breath became erratic, she kissed Martha softly on the lips and then she let out an uncontrolled groan. Her hands relaxed, held still for a moment and then she withdrew them. She straightened Martha's gown and tidied up her own habit and then left the room. Martha was left alone with no blanket or bed. As Martha huddled in a corner shivering and alone, still with that aching in her groin, she felt confused and betrayed but she hoped something good might result from this and that she could endure this treatment.

Later that night, Sister Sencia opened the door, the sister, addressing her as Sarah, told her to dress in her street clothes. Sister Sencia escorted her to the rear door of the convent and as she handed Martha the leather handbag and a small box said "Mother Superior must have loved you". Sister Sencia opened the door and directed Sarah out. As she walked confused and scared into the dark cold night, the Sister said "As Ruth found the path of rightness so might you, may God forgive you".

the best things just happen

Day 2 Meeting Gregoria

A rather loud knocking at the entrance door awoke me from a deep sleep. I had fallen asleep behind the bar still in my street clothes. Wow I can't believe I did that and what a dream, I hope it was a dream. Anyway, who the hell is knocking at my door? Can't they read? It is clearly posted " Closed Until Further Notice". I put the coins back in the safe with the other stuff, remnants of the past.

So standing at the entrance was a beautiful young woman, at my age they all look young, looking like some kind of a CEO. Her attire was one of those business looking outfits, as if you took a man's blue pinstripe suit, disassembled and reassembled to fit a woman. Any way she would look good in any attire. She struck me as being of Italian descent, dark brown hair, which was pulled tightly in a bun in the rear of her head, offset with olive color skin , possibly foreign. "Can I help you?" I asked. I noticed that she took a small step backward; perhaps it was the appearance, slept in clothes, needing a shave or maybe I just had bad breath but whatever she was not impressed with my appearance.

She started to introduce herself " I am Gregoria ...." I stopped her and said "please get to the point." I was tired and not in the mood for any sales pitch. She smiled, an annoyed smile and handed me a large villa envelope. She looked directly into my eyes just for a moment, I had not noticed how beautiful but scary her amber colored eyes were, I felt my knees give slightly and then I heard her say as she departed, "please call me if you're interested". I could detect an accent, maybe German, nodding my head in acknowledgement.

The manila envelope contains an offer to buy the Tavern, all cash. The offer stipulated "AS IS" condition. It was an anonymous offer typed on the standard real estate form. Wow I thought, just what the doctor ordered, I can make my getaway. All I have to do now is plan my escape. I took a closer look at the AS IS condition. The offer had only one stipulation, a 30 day closing. The only thing of interest in the whole place for me was the personal family items in the safe. And I did not know why, I guess it was some sort of gilt. The 30 day close would be no problem.

I no sooner finished reading the sales offer then the phone began to ring. I wondered, who in the hell would be calling me. I don't believe anyone knows I am here. The voice on the other end was that of a man with a Spanish accent. He immediately launched into his spiel, " I am Bemjamond Brovana, a coin collector. I understand you have thirteen silver coins. I might be interested in buying them."

"Excuse me, who are you?" "I am Bemjamond Brovana, a coin collector."

"No No who are you?, how did you get my phone number? And what makes you think I've got silver coins?" I replied.

"Yea, that is a long story but I am confident that it is accurate. I am wondering if you would be willing to bring them by my shop this afternoon? I would like to examine the coins and if they are as I've been told, I have a buyer. In any case you can learn a great deal about the coins."

That afternoon I decided to visit Brovana's coin shop . It was located in the Mission district near old Dolores Mission. I had always liked visiting the Mission. I enjoyed imagining how the area looked back in the day, before the city even existed. I would check out the small cemetery, read the dates, 1803-1847 and wonder about their lives during the (-) dates. It was one of the last of Father Serra's missions. I envision Dolores Street as a rutted dirt road with mule drawn carts. I imagined the surrounded San Francisco hills covered with gold colored dry wild oats. The coin shop was not far from the mission. It was located in what doubled as the basement apartment. The building was one of those once beautiful Victorian buildings that had seen better days.

The interior of the shop, really just a basement apartment with a counter near the entrance and a screen off sleeping quarters in the rear, had the musky smell you would expect. But the shopkeeper was not what I expected rather than an old man wearing powerful dirty glasses, the keeper was a young man smartly dressed. His appearance was more scholarly than a shopkeeper.

After an extensive examination under a microscope the shopkeeper looked up, momentarily stared at the coin, said "Yes, I am sure this coin is one of thirteen coins of the Las Arras my buyer is looking for." I detected a slight German accent as he continued "the coin was minted in Mexico, and most likely shipped to Spain sometime in the 16th century. Eventually they were included in a Las Arras that was part of a dowry given to the Order when a young woman became a nun. You see when a woman becomes a nun she is marrying Jesus and dowry was her father's gift. I believe thirteen coins were in the Las Arras given to the Order of St. Ursula. The Order has been searching for the Las Arras for over a hundred years. During a turbulent period in Prussia the Order transferred the Las Arras to their American convent in New Orlean for safe keeping."

"A what?" I asked.

" LasArras is a traditional wedding gift. It is a small wooden box that contains thirteen silver coins". He explained "The legend has it that a poor Peruvian boy wished to marry a wealthy girl could only offer thirteen silver coins as a dowry but pledge his undying love. So the thirteen coins has become a symbol of unyielding love. These thirteen coins are special because of the individuals involved." The shopkeeper replied. He continued to stare at the coin and without looking up asked " do you have all thirteen? The buyer will pay handsomely for all thirteen but there must be all thirteen." he added.

Things were getting weird I thought to myself, first the dream, then an offer to buy the saloon and now someone wants to buy the coins with the fancy box. I had a feeling that the box was Sarah's?

Chapter 2

Jack and Sarah Saga

The Meeting New Orleans 1854

Sarah in her street clothes holding her leather purse and the fancy box with thirteen coins was sitting on the corner of Chartres and Ursuline streets in New Orleans, alone, cold and confused. The sun was just breaking through the morning mist. A young man stopped and asked her if she needed any help. He was so handsome and well dressed.

He had an air of competency about him. He was obviously of European descent, medium height, with light brown hair, a large nose, and those beautiful eyes. His eyes were steel gray and did not divert quickly, rather they seemed to study their object. Perhaps because she was emotionally vulnerable at that moment or perhaps it was fate but in a short period she fell in love with him. He was young, generous and so alive. He was kind, considerate and so gentile. He taught her that a man could love passionately and yet be sensitive.

She shared a room with Jack and his gambling partner David. They, Jack and David seemed to be more them gambling partners, almost soul mates. Jack told her how he'd met David in Tennessee and how David had helped him survive. David had taught him how to gamble, to spot marks and to read body language. He told Sarah how they had drifted together, working gambling houses up and down the Trace to Natchez. They now work the River Boats that travel between Natchez and New Orleans. Jack was so sure he'd strike it rich one day, how he'd win that big pot and live happily ever afterward.

Jack incorporated Sarah into their endeavor. She'd travel with them helping set up marks with alcohol and when necessary her company including lying with them. She knew this was prostituting herself but she could endure it as long as she could be with Jack. When they would hit a good spell, the three of them, Sarah, Jack and David would celebrate. They would celebrate with food, wine and sometimes dancing. Sarah loved dressing up in store-bought-dresses and fancy hats. She almost felt like the Sarah of old. Sarah would take turns dancing with Jack and David but Jack was her man.

It was Jack that came up with the California idea. He'd heard how a man could strike it rich in the west. They had built up some money and Jack had heard about some used mining equipment in Mexico that could be bought for pennies on the dollar. He said that he could sell it in California at a good profit. This was his ticket and he was going with or without them. David said he always wanted to go west and Sarah was going anywhere Jack went.

Sunday Morning 1857

The clincher was an event in Jackson Square in front of the Cathedral of St Louis. Sarah and David were crossing the Square on their way home after collecting a gambling debt in the Vieux Carré. Debt collection was David's specialty. Sarah often tagged alone especially if the Vieux Carré was the destination, she loved to shop there. It was a beautiful cool fall Sunday morning, a reprieve from the stiffening heat of summer. She noticed some people exiting the church. They were dressed in their Sunday fineness. She realized that it was Sunday, she did not pay much attention to Sundays any longer. She thought about how her family would attend mass every Sunday here in the Square. Sarah preferred the smaller quaint old Cathedral of her youth. It had been enlarged, updated and now too grand for her taste.

Sarah recognized two of the people. It was her aunt and uncle and they were walking in her direction. She had not seen them since her aunt had left her at the convent. Sarah had no intention of acknowledging them until her eyes met theirs. First the uncle's and then the aunt's. She could see the recognition spread over their faces and then something exploded inside her. The years of resentment flowed over her and she looked directly in her aunt's eyes "you bitch, you thieves" She stared at her aunt for a long moment and then she looked at her uncle and said, "She only stole my family's property, you stole my virginity, my innocence and childhood". Her aunt slapped Sarah in the face and Sarah returned the slap, more like a punch, knocking her to the ground, petticoats and all. Her black leather bound bible skidded across the hard stone surface; her hat flipped to one side. Sarah's uncle startled at first, reacted by punching Sarah in the chest knocking her backward. David stepped in to the hostilities and struck the uncle several times knocking him to the ground.

This was no small affair in those times and that city. There was a code of honor to be upheld. These actions, if one was to keep his honor, called for reprisals. Justice was handed out largely based upon social status. David was considered to be a man of color and Sarah a woman of the night. David and Sarah were of the lowest social status so the uncle was free to deal with them as he wished, including having them both hung.

As he vowed to get revenge, a crowd began to gather, mostly onlookers. They were confused and had not taken a position. The citizens of New Orleans were not above mob justice, David knew they had to get out of there and he seized the opportunity. With Sarah in tow, he pushed through the crowd and headed toward the Irish shanty town near the river dock area. The Irish there had little use for New Orleans authority and no tolerance for their high hat aristocratic attitude. The Irish, the refugees, the immigrant workers did the dirty dangerous work, work too dangerous to risk valuable African slaves on.

They reached the assembly of shacks just north of the channel, where present day Canal Street starts, and quickly disappeared in the maze. It was Sunday and the narrow makeshift streets were crowded with families enjoying a brief respite in their horrific lives. While it was clear that they were not part of the Irish clan, it was clear that they were refugees. They were given shelter and protection as the underdogs, something dear to the Irish heart. The shanty town would only provide temporary shelter; the mob would regroup and return in force. David arranged for passage to

Algiers across the river. From there they got a message to Jack. They agreed to meet him and then they all would board a schooner bound for Vera Cruz.

Day 3 Making The Adjustment.

I had considered renting a room nearby, North Beach still had a number of rent by the day rooms, but I decided instead to use the living quarters above the Tavern. To reach it you had to use the steep stair in the rear of the bar area. A small sleeping room at the top of the steppes was one of my favorite places in the building. The room had provided the bar-keeps a safe place to sleep for the night. In the early days, San Francisco nighttime streets were downright dangerous. Thugs and Shanghaiers roamed the waterfront area streets. The sleeping room eliminates the need to leave the relative safety of the saloon late at night.

So I grab my sea bag with all my worldly possessions, climb the age worm steps into a forgotten world. The area had not been used for a long time, the small old bunk was still there and the cold water sink still worked. The area had a musky smell of age and forlorn. I opened the small window above the sink and wondered "why am I doing this, sleeping here when I can afford to rent a room down the street." But regardless I seemed to have a compelling need to stay here.

Again the feeling of being home swept over me. I wondered how many of my ancestors had slept here. I turned over the thin mattress to a slightly clearer side and thought " what the hell it was good enough for them, it's good enough for me." Over the years I'd slept in worse places. It had been quite a day, I was tired and thought " I'll just lay down and rest for a moment."

Day 4 Still in my street clothes

A loud knocking at the entrance door awoke me. I had fallen asleep on the old bunk in my street clothes. The sun filtered by the morning fog streamed through the small dirty window above the sink. Wow I can't believe I slept through the whole night and still in my street clothes, man I must look rough. Who the hell is knocking on my door? It is clearly posted " Closed Until Further Notice". I splashed cold water on my face, straightened my clothes and descended the steep steps " wait a minute I am coming." I shouted.

At the entrance agin was that beautiful young woman, She was dressed in another neat business looking outfit. Her dark brown hair freshly pulled tightly in a bun in the rear of her head. She's beautiful but dangerous I thought as I asked "what do you want?" After a momentary pause while observing my unkempt appearance "Oh, just a little of your time". She replied "I'll bet a lot more," I thought.

"If you please, I would like to discuss the terms of purchase" she said as she looked at me with those gorgeous eyes. I detected a slight smile seeping through her otherwise serious business persona.

"Can I come in, out of the cold and discuss the purchase offer?" she asked.

Reluctantly "ok but the place is a mess" I answered.

I brushed off, the best I could, a couple of chairs and a table near the entrance.

Then I said " what's to discuss, it a as-is cash offer" I asked. She laid a sheet of paper on the table with a bunch of typed legal looking verbiage on it. That is when I realized this was the, "will not take no for an answer" visit.

As she got into her pitch about how great an offer this is and what a contribution the planned redevelopment would make to the community my attention diverted to the painting hanging on the wall , a painting of an almost nude lady with a hundred years worth of dust, smoke and time caked on its surface. My uncle said he'd heard that the woman was his Grandmother, the owner of the Bella Union, a bar and dancehall in the old Barbary Coast that had closed long ago. Then I began to think about the long line of ancestors that had owned the Tavern and realized that I did not know their names. I did not know which ancestor started this whole saloon business.

About this time the young lady finished her pitch with " time is of the essence here, are ready to sign the docs and get on with sale?"

I must have looked like a deer caught in the headlights, I was so surprised by her demand. "Well, I'll consult my board of directors," I said jokingly. "Seriously, I will need a few days to make a decision."

After she left, I dug out the buy offer and began to read the details but my mind drifted off to the painting, the lady, the time and the ancestors. I recalled the receipt for three passages to California. Jack, David and Sarah.

Chapter 3
Faithful only to thyself

Gilchrist Fergus Erskine (Jack) 1835-1906

Gilchrist, but always called Jack, was born to a Catholic Scottish immigrant family in West Virginia. No one quite knew why he was called Jack but no one outside his family knew his given name. That was just fine with Jack; the last thing he wanted was to be called Gilchrist. His father, Eoin, left Scotland in 1815 at fourteen as an indentured servant to a family in Virginia. Upon completion of the term of indentureship, he worked as a teamster hauling freight to the new settlement in the Appalachian in western Virginia. Eoin was a rightist man, God fearing, hardworking and did not drink or squander his money. After purchasing a plot of land in hills above the Ohio Valley, Eoin went about the business of acquiring a wife. He decided that only a good Christian Scottish woman would do. So he sent his second cousin, Fiona, to join him in marriage. They built a cabin on his land and began farming.

Every other spring a child would come like clockwork. Eoin claimed it would be every spring if not for Fiona nursing her babies. Folklore had it that while nursing a woman could not conceive. Fiona said that if it were not for baby teeth, she'd nurse her babies for years. By the time Jack was thirteen, the family had grown to number eleven and existed on beans, corn and wild game. One of Jack's chores, in addition to help with the farming was to forage the nearby woods for food. Jack had become quite skillful at catching small game and collecting berries and bird eggs. The Choctaw squaw that lived with the old Frenchmen down the road had taught him to build traps from twigs. She showed him how to trap birds and rodents. Jack had no formal teaching and only a little home learning, but his natural intelligence and keen observation set him apart from most locals. Jack knew in his heart that he did not want to live his life as a dirt farmer; that he did not want to be child poor like his father; that his father's God was not his; that he would only prune from life the things that served him.

No Farewell

His parents worked tirelessly to support the family but with their meager holding, were only able to provide a subsistence living. At whit's end, they made a decision that one of the children had to go. They felt that they needed the oldest, Thomas, to help in the farming and therefore the second oldest, Jack should go. His father talked about an indentureship as a servant. Jack would have none of it, he had no intention of being a servant, indentured or not. By nature, Jack would rather risk it all and live on his terms than to ever be indentured to anything.

Jack told his parents that he was striking out on his own and that they could not stop him. His father was sad and his mother cried. This is not the life that they come to America for.

Before the sun rose the next morning, Jack started out dressed in his best and warmest homespun and headed out with his bedroll. Inside the bedroll was a pair of moccasins and some rations. He wore a broad brim hat to protect his face from the strong spring sun. A 6-inch blade knife in a rawhide sheath was strapped to his waist. For the knife and moccasins, he'd trade three grouse eggs and two rabbits to the squaw.

He did not say goodbye to his brothers and sisters. His parents were already out of the cabin attending to the corn field. His mother and father were seeding before the sunrise. They'd seed a small section then quickly cover it with earth to protect the seeds from the crows. The family's survival depended on the corn crop and the birds were one of many threats to it. His mother stopped seeding and walked over to him and kissed a small

Ivory Irish Cross and gave it to him. His father stopped and looked his way and said "may god go with thee, goodbye Jack ". His mother slowly turned away and returned to her work. She did not say a word.

The sun was rising in the east as Jack headed down the trail leading to the nearby westward flowing creek. When the local farmer took their goods to market they'd follow this creek. Jack followed the creek that he was told would lead to a bigger creek and then eventually to the Cumberland River. He thought about his older brother, Thomas. He envisioned Thomas spending years of toil helping the family scrape out a living on that lowly plot of land. How glad he was to be on this way, never to turn another dirt sod. Jack saw his god-fearing father as foolish and swore he'd be different.

The Half Breed David Mc Lish 1810-1867

David, known locally as the half breed Mc Lish, was not technically a half breed. He was really only one forth Indian. His father, Gregory was of English German descent. His mother was half Chickasaw, half French.

David was told that his grandfather had been a Hessian officer enlisted to fight for George the III during the revolutionary war and had chosen to remain in Canada. David's grandmother had been a royalist and fled with her family to Canada during that war. It was not clear how his grandparents got together or what became of them but by 1802 David's father was operating a Stand on the Natchez Trace. David's mother died giving birth to him. David's father never talked much about her. David was mostly raised by Chickasaw squaws that lived near the Stand.

While David was only part Chickasaw, his appearance and manor were largely Indian. He'd acquired his father's large, over six feet tall, muscular frame and his mother's straight jet black hair, intensely black eyes and high cheekbones. He was fluent in three native tongues as well as English. He had no formal education and was all but illiterate. But he was well versed in the ways of survival.

Locally he was known as a liar and a cheat. But David did not see any dishonor here. He was taught early that stealing was a necessary part of life. "Did not the wolf steal the coyote's kill to feed its young?" he would ask. And then add "Did not the Yankees tell the Chickasaws they only wanted to use the Trace, but in fact wanted to steal it, their land, their honor, their pride"?

By the time David was a young man, the hay days of the Trace were over. The steam driven riverboats now handled the majority of the traffic. The once busy and dangerous Trace was now used mostly by locals. David's father had moved on years ago leaving David to fend for himself. Only a few Stands were still operating. David continued to operate the McLish Stand the best he could. His main source of income now was alcohol, gambling and whoring.

There were a number of squaws in the area that were reduced to prostituting to make a living. They were the unwanted squaws, either too ugly or too old to be wanted. They were the remnants of the once proud and mighty Chickasaw nation, left behind after the Great Chickasaw Cession, the treaty that opened up west Tennessee for legal settlement, the final act of sealing the land. He would provide the squaws to his customers for a cut of the fee. He did not see this as morally wrong, simply providing a service to his customers as well as helping the unwanted squaws.

David's gambling skills were limited and mostly he'd prey upon the occasional unsuspecting traveler. With the help of the squaws he'd liquor them up and cheater them out of their money. He used marked cards, dealing from the bottom of the deck and a spotter to cheat them. David was careful not to win too many hands, only the higher stake ones. David was not above using physical force and threats when necessary to handle the occasional wise guy that caught on. Dave saw this not as a test of his manhood or pride but only as a necessary aspect of the business.

Jack's Education 1848

Jack had spent a hard six months since leaving home. Finding food was tough and getting tougher as spring gave way to summer. He'd worked his way down the Cumberland River to Nashville. He hung around a few days then headed southwest on the Trace. On the third day out, he noticed a man and two boys or perhaps a boy and a girl, at the edge of the woods near the Trace. They were poorly dressed with dirty faces and unkempt hair. The man had a scar from his ear to the corner of his mouth. They were standing to one side of the Trace and as Jack walked past, they looked him over. They looked too long, the man in particular. He seemed to be measuring Jack. Jack would never forget that look. Jack now understood and recognized that he was being marked. He'd been told that victims were almost always marked first.

They must have known the area well because they managed to skirt through the woods and get ahead of Jack. The boy or girl, Jack could not tell which, was standing on the road's edge and as Jack approached the person, Jack decided it was a girl. She asked Jack for directions. Jack did not see the blow coming, he assumed the man had sneaked up behind as the girl was talking. He was knocked to the ground. As he laid there stunned but semiconscious, they quickly took his bed roll, his hat and his new moccasins. They demanded money and when Jack could not provide any, they took it out of his hide. Jack kind of felt that they preferred it that way, as if Jack had to pay for something but he did not know what. One thing for sure Jack thought, he'd be more observant in the future, that he would be no one's easy mark again.

Jack never understood why they did not take his knife and sheath, perhaps they intended to but ran out of time and quickly disappeared into the woods at the sound of an approaching wagon. Jack recognized the native tongue of the Chickasaw, the same language his neighbor's squaw spoke. The squaws claimed out of the wagon and lifted Jack up with surprising ease and dumped him like a sack of potatoes in the back of the wagon. As Jack laid moaning in a fetal position, the squaws climbed in next to Jack and the wagon started slowly down the road.

The squaws began to talk softly between them in their native tongue. They spoke in a whisper so that the driver could not hear and in their native tongue so Jack could not understand. The older of the two asked" what are we going to do with his young coyote"? The younger squaw replied "I suppose to nurse him". The older one replied "I'd rather cook him for dinner, he looks real tender." They both laughed. Then the younger looked at Jack and said" maybe I will use him to stay warm at night" The older one replied" good then he can run away like your husband". "Oh and where is yours" Shouted the younger one. The driver turned and said "if you two keep it up you will be walking to the Stand".

It was evening when they arrived at the Stand. The driver told Jack that he could bunk with the Squaws for the night. Given Jack's condition and options, he accepted the offer. But he thought he'd not be a squaw's sleeping partner.

The squaws lived in a dugout in the bank at the rear of the Stand. The front of the dugout was closed off by some old wooden planks held together by rawhide straps. The end plank could be moved and functioned as the door. In the rear of the dugout were a few animal hides spread over some more wooden planks resting on round logs a foot or so above ground. Though this did not seem like much of a bed, it was a welcome sight to Jack. Jack was cold, tired, hurting and he crawled into bed without anything to eat or speaking a word.

It was early summer and the nights on the Trace were quite cold. By early morning the frost was on the ground. That night seemed particularly cold. Perhaps it was Jack's condition but for whatever reason Jack could not stop shivering.

Jack could not seem to get enough hide covering him to get warm. Some time that night the old squaw crawled under the hides next to him and held him tightly against her body. Her warmth spread through his body and after a moment he stopped shivering and in his best Chickasaw, he said "thank you" and fell into a deep sleep.

Day 5 Another Night in Street Clothes

I was determined not to fall asleep and spend another night sleeping in street clothes so I decided to rent a room for the night. But first I wanted to look at the stuff, the letter from my uncle and a small leather bonded journal in the safe. I sat at the bar and began to read the letter from my uncle. It contained a list of the owner of the Tavern along with some other family details. At the head of the list of owners was a name of someone I had never heard of, Nickelas Wegner.

Chapter 4
1854 The Voyage

Nickelas Wagner 1823

Nickelas Wagner of the Mosel Valley, present day Germany but then it was part of France. After the Great War, WW1, The area became known as Alsace Lorraine region. Nickelas, who was an almost ancestor, is 31years old and works in the family tavern. The family is noted locally for two things: beer brewing and a mixed marriage. The family has been brewing beer for many generations; since the Roman occupation it was said. This mixed marriage stuff started with his father, Lloyd. He married a French woman, Maria Tintinger. This mixed marriage was a big deal in a region so thoroughly divided by languages, French and German. The control of Mosel Valley has switched between the Prussians and the Franks ever since the Roman retreated fourteen hundred years before. They'd spilled many a young man's blood over this land and were not about to forget it. Their standard bearer in modern times was their language because except for language there was no way to tell a Prussian from a Frank.

Two good things came out of this mixed marriage, Nickelas learned to fight and to speak both French and German fluently. Nickelas was not a good-looking man; he was short and stocky with massive forearms, stout legs and a neck like a bull. His dark brown hair was stiff and refused to be controlled. His face was heavily scarred with pock marks from a childhood case of the chicken pocks. His blue eyes though were soft and warm and quick to smile. They betrayed his true nature, intelligent and loving. He was not tall and attractive like his older brother, Fredric and the town's people said that he was a throwback to some Roman and of course the French speaking people said it was from the Prussian father and the German speaking people claimed it came from the French mother.

While it is true that Nickelas was valued for his brewing skill, his main contribution was keeping peace in the tavern. These were dangerous days with another Franco Prussian war on the horizon. The young men were already siding up and Nickelas's main task was to keep it out of the tavern. It was not long before Nickelas had a reputation as a no- nonsense man and one not to be confronted. It was said that he'd thrown three burly young Prussian boys out of the tavern and when they continued to protest, he gave all three a beating to remember. Nickelas was the third child of this union which put him out of the inheritance picture regarding the family business. While his tough reputation helped maintain peace in the tavern and earned respect from the village men, it did nothing to enhance his appeal to the women. With no prospect of a lover and a chance of being forcibly recruited for another war, Nickelas decided to seek his fortune elsewhere.

Never To Return

In the fall of 1854 Nickelas said goodbye to his Father, Mother, Sister and Brother and set off for Hamburg. As he was leaving the family tavern with his meager belongings, his mother handed him a small leather bag and kissed him on the cheek. She had not kissed his cheek like that since he was a small child. She did not say a word but they both understood that it was the last kiss from his mother and that they would never meet again.

Hamburg was a thriving port city located on the confluence of the rivers Elbe, Bille and Alster. Nickelas quickly found employment at a local brewery. The brewery was near the waterfront area. There were many inexpensive rooming houses in the area. They were frequented by sailors, peddlers and working women. Nickelas was relatively happy there. With his wages he could buy bread and cheese and the beer he got free, more or less, as a bonus from his job. With the free beer and a little money he could secure the company of a working lady for the night. In his home village his nights had always been lonely since he was neither attractive nor wealthy enough to gain the affection of the young ladies and there were no working ladies in the village, that type of woman was not tolerated there.

The working women of Hamburg filled his bed almost every night. He loved their softness, their smell, their affection and he felt good about providing them security, even if it was only for that night. He developed a relationship with one special young lady and she became a regular visitor to his room. Her name was Hildegard but she was called Silky, because of her milk white smooth skin. There was an unspoken agreement between them; they never discussed the past nor the future. There were only the nights together.

In the waterfront taverns, Nickelas met sailors from all over the world. They had grand stories about faraway places like Japan, India. Stories of grand brothels with many young women in beautiful gowns to choose from. But to Nickelas this sounded like a tavern with too many beers to choose from when all he really wanted was one good one to enjoy.

Hamburg which had been a free city for centuries was annexed by France under Napoleon but with his defeat in1815 and the establishment of the German Confederation, the city was once again a Free City with complete control of its affairs. By1855 the whole of Europe was politically unstable. There had been peasant revolts against the establishment throughout France and Germany. There was talk about another war with France. Hamburg felt the need to strengthen their military, perhaps because of the outside factors or internal unrest. It is always a good political ploy to have an external enemy to divert attention from your internal issues.

And so the powers-to-be ordered the army to begin recruiting troops. The Army would routinely sweep through areas gathering up fighting age men, particularly men without local roots. The waterfront area was a prime place to find such people. Silky and the other working women always seemed to know about pending sweeps and would warn the men. But Nickelas knew that there was a bounty to be paid for men like him and felt that it would be only a matter of time till someone betrayed him and he'd be caught and forced to join the army.

The Passage

One morning after sharing his bed with Silky, she told him he must not return to the room, that he'd been targeted by the local master at arms and would be forced into service that evening. She'd gotten it via the women's grapevine, after all the master of arms was a regular customer. She told Nickelas not to travel over land. In those days traveling in the German Confederation without the proper papers was a sure way of ending up in the infantry, a potential death sentence.

The only other route was by sea but with no sea experience, it would be difficult to escape as a sailor and he did not have the money to pay for passage. Silky told him about a Norwegian captain who was looking for sailors. She only knew him as Norwegian Red, he had bright red hair. Nickelas had heard of him; he had a reputation as a drinker and gambler. He owned an 17th century merchant sailing ship, a square- sailed cog, Keeping it afloat required a lot of luck, good seamanship and a good bilge pump with strong men to operate it. Most experienced sailors were reluctant to sail on such a ship.

Silky told him that the Norwegian was setting sail on the next high tide. No one knew his destination but she felt that this was his best chance of escaping. Nickelas packed his meager belongings, including the little leather bag and set off intent on sailing with the Norwegian.

Nickelas waited for the right moment, just before the gang plank would be pulled, he boarded the ship. The Norwegian, who seemed to expect him, directed Nickelas below and it became clear that Silky had made some kind of arrangement. It was a long, hard, cold voyage. The Northern Gail was quite seaworthy for a 17 century ship but still required constant bilge pump manning.

The bilge pump crew stood a four-hour watch, physically demanding for even young men but Nickelas now in his thirties was up to the task to the surprise of his younger shipmates. The Norwegian Captain took a North Atlantic route, rather dangerous not heavily traveled this time of the year, as if their destination was somewhere in North America. It would have been safer and easier to sail though the English Channel down the French coast, pick up western trade winds and then across the Atlantic. It seems that the Norwegian was involved in smuggling and part of the ploy was to disguise his ship as old, not worthy of attention and take less used sea routes.

A few days at sea and the scuttlebutt had it that the cargo was munitions destined for the Mexican rebels. They would have to run the French embargo to get there. If the French intercepted the shipment, the captain would be hung and the crew surely imprisoned. Still Nickelas preferred his situation to that of being in the infantry, a sure death sentence.

Day 6 A Person Standing

*T*he next day as I was walking down Grant St, returning from my morning coffee, I noticed a person standing in front of the Tavern. As I got closer I recognized it was Gregoria, so beautiful standing there, I assumed she was going to hassle me about the sale of the property. She was not dressed in her CEO outfit but rather in a pullover sweater and jeans. Her hair was allowed to fall freely and fell gently over her shoulders.

She said , "I knew your family. I was raised in the neighborhood and my family have roots here in North Beach. We have had many family celebrations, my christening, my sister baby shower, my father's retirement, in the Tavern. Your mother was a great person and a fine host. When she passed and the Tavern was closed, it felt like part of me was lost."

I was at loss for words, all the memories of my family flooded by my consciousness and my eyes began to water. I began to think about all those years I had been gone. A mixed feelings of loss, regret and guilt overwhelmed me. I was a rebel without a clue, I was determined not to live in the umbrella of my family. I was going places but had no idea where or any plans, so I joined the Navy. I just wanted to escape. "My Grandmother knew your family well", she continued. "She would tell me stories of how ship's crews would abandon their ships and run off to the gold fields in the Sierras. She said the ship that Nickelas, one of original owners, came on was abandoned and buried under the waterfront".

Chapter 5
California

The crew and the passenger alike could smell land as the Northern Gail approached the California coast. It is true that one can smell land after being at sea for a while. Have you ever smelled a new plowed field? well that is the smell mixed with mankind presence.

The Northern Gail, an obsolete 17 century merchant marine ship. These ships were commonly referred to as the coffin fleet. These ships could be bought for almost nothing. The trick was to keep them afloat long enough to make some money. There were a number of these old ships that had seen better days and sailors did not like to crew them. She had been at sea for six months. She had left Vera Cruz with a load of mining equipment and three, two men and a woman. She had to sail around the tip of South America, through the Straits of Magellan. It had been tough going and it took all the seamanship of the captain and some luck to hold the old ship on course and afloat.

Entering the bay through the narrow gate with treacherous currents also took a bit of seamanship. The bay itself was large and a fine refuge for weary ships and crews. The southern shore of the harbor was clogged with abandoned ships and seemed more like a graveyard than a mooring. Beyond that laid the bustling young city of San Francisco. Just a decade ago it had been a little sleepy Mexican village, Yerba Buena with a couple hundred inhabitants.

Lieutenant Bartlett as the acting Alcalde had changed its name to match the bay. The Gold Rush of 49 caused a population explosion and by 1856 it had become the largest city west of the Mississippi. The city was young; its residents young, adventurous, ambitious and dangerous. Into this fray the three passengers, the French beer brew master and the crew seeking adventure and their fortunes.

San Francisco was to be Northern Gail's final destination. The Northern Gail was not her original name, the Norwegian captain had renamed her that. When she entered service in 1747, as the Dolphin. She was built by the master shipwright in Plymouth England to the rigid standards of Her Majesty's Admiralty. She was commissioned by the East India Company and served that company for thirty years. She had many masters over the years and had sailed around the world. She'd made ports throughout Asia, Africa, Europe and America. After her three passengers, Jack, David, Sarah along with a cargo of mining equipment were unloaded, the crew then abandoned her. The Northern Gail became just another unwanted, tired out ship alongside the multitude of others. It is said that she is buried in the landfill of Yerba Buena cove but no one knows for sure because there's no marker, Northern Gail 1747-1856.

Sarah and Jack San Francisco

Sarah, Jack and David rented a house just south of Black Point. It was one of those prefab houses built in China and shipped to California. Jack and David were busy working the gambling joints at night and working on deals in the daytime. One deal was with some men from Sacramento. A deal Jack said would set them up for life. It evolved trading the mining equipment for shares of mines. Equipment needed for hard rock mines in the Sierra foothills. Sarah was busy being a homemaker and happy even though she long to have a place for just her and Jack. Jack did not notice Sarah's growing stomach but she knew that she was carrying his child.

She felt good and was quite happy about the situation. But when Jack discovered it, his mood turned black and she could do nothing right. He stopped sleeping with her and began staying away from home for extended periods. She hoped that after the child was born, things would return to normal. That Jack would learn to love and protect his baby. But then Jack along with David simply disappeared without a word and Sarah was left to fend for herself. Her only means of support was taken in laundry and a little prostitution. But as she began showing, the prostitution income disappeared and the laundry money dwindled. Finally she could not pay the rent and she was evicted. She was eight months pregnant and living on the street. She'd lost weight, her clothes were tattered and her hair was unkempt but she was determined to stay alive, have his baby and then to find her man.

Chapter 6
A Chance Meeting 1862

Fredric Jack Wagner/ Erskine 1861- 1925

Nickelas did not recognize her at first but after a moment he could see past the ragged clothes, dirty face and unkempt hair. In the flickering gaslights he could see that only a trace of youth remained. She did not seem to notice or recognize him either. Initially he intended to simply walk past her but then he remembered her as she was aboard the Northern Gail, so young and alive. Nickelas had not seen Sarah since they had arrived in San Francisco four years earlier. He'd understood that she was living with her traveling companions. He was surprised now to see her living on the street. He assumed that she had a falling out with Jack since he seemed to be her mate. But still he could not believe she could have changed so much.

It was late December, nearly Christmas, the city was unusually cold, and it seemed as if someone else was speaking as he asked if she needed a place for the night. As he helped her to her feet, he noted that she was pregnant and started regretting his invitation. Oh well he thought, it was only for one night. But by the next morning he began to comprehend the magnitude of her situation, unmarried with a child and no means of support.

While he had concerned for her, the child's wellbeing was utmost to him. He could not in good conscience turn them back on to the street.

As a young man in France he'd seen so many wanted children roaming the countryside, many the product of the Napoleonic wars and some the product of an unwanted pregnancy. He knew he was fortunate to have had the warmth and love of a family. He decided to provide her shelter and support until she had the baby and she was on her feet, both physically and mentally. He would arrange for a Chinese Midwife to assist her.

The Chinese Midwife Yan Qui Lie 1844-1916

Yan Qui Lie was from a northern Chinese province, Jiangsu. It is located on the eastern coast along the Yellow Sea. The mighty Yangtze River flowed through it into the sea. Yan's father was a physician and an herb merchant there. At the time Yan was born, the Qing Dynasty was in disarray with rampant corruption and a steady decentralization of power. Local WarLords ruled as they wished, hunger and sickness run rampant in his china. Qui Lie, her father, did business with merchants that travel the world.

He'd heard stories about the Americas and of Chinese settlements there. He was quite concerned about his children's future. Qui Lie did not understand that China was caught in a clash between its traditions and the need to modernize. From his perspective China had always been the center of the civilized world but be that as it may, China was a dangerous place.

He had two children, a six year old boy and ten year old girl. He, as many Chinese valued his son most but he truly loved his daughter. His son would stay under his protection and his daughter would be sent away to a safer place until things settled here in China. With heavy heart, tears in his eyes, he pinned a note to her jacket as she boarded the Yankee clipper ship heading for Yerba Buena. There was a small Chinese settlement there. An herb merchant, Sing Tin Eli that he knew had opened a store there and could use an assistant. Sing Tin Eli would meet her and take charge of her.

Yan Qui was a bright child and though her native tongue was Mandarin, she quickly picked up both Cantonese and English. From her father she'd learn to administer various Chinese medical treatments and was proficient in assisting childbirth. By the time she was sixteen she had developed in a rather attractive woman. Being from northern China she was taller than the typical Cantonese women with a narrower face, a strong jaw, high cheekbones, shiny straight black hair and intelligent drake brown eyes that caught your attention. In addition to being a healthy and attractive young woman, she was known throughout China Town for her ability to speak English and her medical skills. She was considered special and a marriage arrangement with the prominent politically connected Chinese family was in her future.

In the Chinese tradition in the mid nineteenth century, Yan Qui was the property of Sing Tin Li, Mr. Sing. It was in his right to use her as he wished or even sell her as he wished. Most Chinese women at that time had three options, be a servant, a wife or a prostitute but her medical and language skills set her apart. She was a valuable asset to Mr. Sing and he intended to use her in his business. He would for a price lease her under contract for a period of time.

Such was the case when a laowai (foreigner in Mandarin), contracted to have her services as a midwife. The contract was for three months and since he was a laowai, he'd have to pay two times the fee and in advance.

The Best Laid Plans

Nickelas was surprised and confused by Sarah's behavior after the baby was born. He anticipated her motherly instincts would take hold and she'd start thinking in terms of the baby's wellbeing but as soon as she was able, she started looking for Jack. She'd leave the baby with the Chinese midwife in the morning and not return until late evening. Because the baby was not getting enough milk from Sarah, the midwife, Yan Qui, would buy fresh mother's milk each day in ChinaTown. The baby, a boy, was quite weak at birth, most likely due to the poor physical condition of the mother. Yan Qui was ever so attentive and nursed the child with herbs and love. She called him boa bie since Sarah had not given him a name. Yan Qui would rock him in her arms and sing Chinese lullaby to him ever so softly. She'd warm the mother's milk with her body before feeding him. As time went by Sarah would leave for long periods and by the time the baby was about six weeks old she was gone.

No one including Yan Qui anticipated that she would fall in love with the Nickelas. The smell of baby's hair brought back memories of her brother. She helped her mother care for him and she missed him so. When she held the baby close and felt his warmth, a wonderful feeling of fulfillment would come over her. And sometimes when Nickelas would come every near when taking the baby from her, she'd feel a strong desire to press against his body. She was overwhelmed by Nickelas kindness. She longed to be held in his arms. When she looked deep into his soft blue eyes, she knew that she wanted to stay and be part of his life. But this would be dangerous for everyone involved. In addition to Mr. Sing property rights there was the racial aspect to deal with. Racial tensions were running high in the city between the Chinese and the European communities. Since the end of the gold rush the competition for jobs between them had intensified to the point of open hostility. Since childhood Yan Qui had been taught to deny her feelings, to follow tradition and do her duty as her elder wished. But she was a woman above all else and could not deny her feelings. She made a decision to risk it all.

She would be part of their life or no life. As Sarah's sojourners became ever longer, Nickelas realized that she had no intentions of caring for the baby and that he might be left to care for him. In addition, he did not fully understand the developing crises with the midwife. He greatly appreciated her devotion to the child and was comfortable with her presence. While he felt the desire when close to her, he considered himself to be much too old and besides she was Chinese, a totally different culture, the property of Sing Tin Li. He tried to dismiss any notion of a union between them and ponder the child's situation. In a way, unknown to him, the issue was resolved for him when Yan Qui notified Mr. Sing that she did not want to return. That she intended to care for the child.

She did not tell Mr. Sing of her feelings for Nickelas, only for her devotion to the child.

Mr. Sing's Dilemma

Mr. Sing, unlike many of his countrymen, was a big man by Nineteenth century standards. He always dressed in fine silk traditional Chinese style clothes and was well known not only in ChinaTown but also in the European area of the city. He had established a contracting, contracting Chinese laborers to the American community, business and he'd done quite well.

Mr. Sing was considered to be one of the wealthiest Chinese around. He was born in the Zhongshan area of China in 1820, to a wealthy merchant class family. Historically this class had been restricted and regulated based upon the belief that its pursuit of profit could upset the social balance of the state. Because of the decentralization of power of the Qing Dynasty, trade with the west had opened up and the merchant class experienced unprecedented gain in status and wealth. Sing Tin Li's family traditionally traded along coastal China but with the opening of the west they expanded their trading to the west coast of America.

During the 1830's, the Sing Tin Li family was trading their goods throughout Alta California. By 1843, they had established an herb trading post in the village of Yerba Buena. Sing Tin Li was fond of pointing out that he'd been here before it was San Francisco. Be that as it may, there was currently an especially strong anti Chinese climate in the city. To make the situation worse, Yan Qui was refusing to return and he was in a very difficult position, losing face. He'd promised her father he'd care for her until she was of marrying age; that he'd provide dowry in return for her services. Well of course she was already sixteen, a couple years older than the traditional marriage age but she was such an excellent source of income that he had procrastinated a bit, maybe a bit too long.

Nickelas 's Dilemma

With the baby approaching twelve weeks old, it became crystal clear that Sarah would not be part of his life and Nickelas had to face up to the situation. He grew very fond of the child and had decided that he would care for him as if he was his son. He knew he needed female help and hoped that he could extend Yan Qui's contract. She was doing a fine job and seemed to be strongly attached to the baby. He first needed to discuss this with Yan Qui. He felt that it was important that she was willing to stay awhile longer. Yan Qui could speak excellent English, in fact better than Nickelas. So when Nickelas asked if she would help him for a bit longer, Yan Qui told him yes, that she was not going back ever, that she was a free woman; that she controlled her own destiny and she would stay as long as he wished. There was no doubt as to her wishes.

Late on a raining afternoon, two rough looking Irishmen approached Nickelas behind the bar at the Tavern. Nickelas knew of them because of their trade. They were Shanghai specialists employed by various ship captains to fill their employment requirements. It was well known throughout the area that Nickelas did not tolerate such activities in his tavern, so he was surprised by their presence. Their English was difficult to understand because of a heavy Irish brogue but the message was clear.

Yan Qui was to return to her owner or else. Nickelas had been on the fence regarding Yan Qui but he was not a man to order around. Besides, to him this ownership, slavery stuff was unacceptable. Thousands of men were dying in a war right now to abolish this.

Now the Irishmen's instructions were no rough stuff, only to intimidate Nickelas, but perhaps because of his short stature or perhaps because of their nature they began to shove him about. That was a mistake, Nickelas came over the bar knocking the biggest one back over a table, spattering the evening's, all you can eat for two bits spread of lima beans and sausage stew, in all directions. He proceeded to bear hug the second man and drove him backward out the door, across the wood plank sidewalk on to DuPont Street driving him hard onto the water-soaked manure covered cobblestones street, shattering bystanders, horses and what all; the Irishman hit with such force that it knocked him senseless. Nickelas then returned to the tavern to find the big guy, pretty much covered in the evening spread, just getting to his feet. He grabbed him by the back of his neck and threw him out onto DuPont Street. His intention was to take the fight to the street but the two thugs wanted no part of this crazy German and quickly vanished into the crowd. Now Nickelas was off the fence, Yan Qui could stay as long as she wished.

Diplomacy

Mr. Sing was upset when he heard about the confrontation at the Tavern. With all this anti Chinese stuff raging in the city and this slavery stuff too, he correctly understood that diplomacy was in order. It was clear that Yan Qui was a lost cause, she'd made up her mind to control her own destiny; he could not expect any support from either the Chinese community or the city police. The most important thing was to prevent the confrontation at the Tavern from becoming a full scale race war. Although he had his misgivings about Yan Qui wellbeing, how could she survive and prosper with those foreign devils, he saw that he had no choice but release her and did so via a message and a gift to Nickelas.

The note read "A thousand apologies for the misunderstanding. I give you Yan Qui as my gift and hope you understand that her future is now in your hands. Your lowly and humble servant Sing Tin Li".

He still had the Irish thugs that he'd hired and Yan Qui father to deal with. So as an experienced trader he set out to make the appropriate deals. Cash was sufficient regarding the Irish thugs but Yan father required a promise to watch over Yan and if necessary welcome her back to the Chinese community with an open heart.

So in the span of twelve weeks Nickelas went from being a single tavern operator to a man responsible for a child and a young Chinese woman. His mother always said everything happens for the best and he sure hoped this was the case here. At any rate, he would make the best of this situation. He initially envisioned going about his life as before with Yan Qui taking care of the child But he found his life becoming more and more intertwined with theirs. He'd spend his mornings helping Yan Qui care for the child, which he started calling Fredric. For the first time in a long time Nickelas felt the warmth of a family. Nearly fifty one, with a short lifetime in the 1800s he was considered a bit long on the tooth but perhaps just old enough now to appreciate those things family life brought.

Day 7 Businessman

*T*he old leather bound notebook in the safe had a number of gold mining stock listed. Gregoria's grandmother has told her story about sailors jumping ships in the old days to rush off to search for gold in the Sierras. I wonder if the notebook had been accidentally lost in the saloon. I decided to take a closer look and see if some long ago owner's name is there. To my surprise I found a name that is becoming familiar now, Jack Erskine, one of the saloon's owners I believe.

a gold mine is a hole with a liar at the bottom

"Mark Twain"

Chapter 7
The Businessman

Jack's Revelation 1861

When Jack found out that Sarah was with child, all he could think about was a life in poverty, a life like his parents, child poor. Jack had come to the conclusion that gambling with cards and dice was not that profitable and a rather dangerous trade, especially in San Francisco.

But there was another game, mining stocks, in town that was more to his liking, more lucrative and less dangerous. To jack the stock market was just another scam, another way to cheat at the game. There was no hotter market in 61 then Virginia City. He'd been working a deal with a group of Sacramento businessmen. David and he were the point men in the deal. Their job was to find or establish mining claims in the Virginia City area that the businessmen in turn could market. The claims did not have to be big products, just enough of a claim to be legally sold as mining stock. Of course legally at that time was quite subjective since there were no governing boards but then the only real goal of the governing board is to gain sufficient respect to stay in business and out of jail or worse yet, shot by an irate customer.

To Jack's surprise, he soon discovered that he had a knack for this stock business; that he could sort through the perspective offers and select the better then average claim. As he became successful and built up a reputation as an honest businessman, he started to operate more as a stock broker, buying and selling stock as well as establishing initial offerings. With success came independence from the Sacramento group and status with the Virginia City business community. For the first time in this life, Jack felt like part of the establishment. He rented a fine apartment in the International Hotel, attended fashionable social functions and hobnobbed with the city's elite. Virginia City seemed custom made for Jack and he planned to make it his home. Here he saw his chance to become a man of substance with all fringe benefits, property, money, power and perhaps a beautiful wife.

Soldier's Destiny
Addison Jefferson Whitfield 1844 -1867

Addison was born into a well-established southern family. His grandfather had been a revolutionary soldier and had fought alongside General Daniel Morgan in the battle at Cowpens, South Carolina in1781. Addison grew into a fine looking young man, like Michelangelo's David, tall and straight with a strong brutally handsome face topped with blond wavy hair, idealized southern gentlemen. His family had originally been in the tobacco growing business but had migrated into the banking side of that business. He showed little interest in banking business and so this father sent him to the Marion Military Institute in Alabama, to study engineering. He did not do well in engineering for his real love was hunting and riding horses. His father had won him an appointment at West Point but with all the talk about the coming war he showed no interest there.

His father, who was an abolitionist, urged him to attend West Point and become a union officer but many of his classmates and friends were enlisting with the Confederate forces and so just before his seventeenth birthday he left school to join the Confederate Army. He endured the war mostly bivouacked in various rural outposts. He was an excellent hunter and was assigned to the Quarter Master's squad. His specialty was providing fresh meat either wild or domestic. When not hunting, he played poker with his fellow soldiers. He had a real knack for reading facial expressions and body language. He became efficient at sending subtle false signals and then reading his opponents reaction. He found this to be a powerful asset and more often than not he'd be ahead at the game's end. He felt that gambling was the life for him.

In April 65 his squad was involved in a small engagement with Sherman's advance force. He proved to be a cunning adversary and quite cool under fire. There had been hand to hand fighting and many of this cohort were lost. But one battle was sufficient for him. He could see that the cause was lost and when General Hill called for a retreat, he just ducked into the nearby woods to wait for Sherman's main force to pass. By chance a young confederate captain, badly wounded, had also ducked into the woods.

Addison tried to help him to no avail and he quietly died. Addison removed his good warm wool blood-stained overcoat and his side arm, after all, the captain had no use for them now. It was a dangerous gamble he'd taken, he could end up being shot by either side but luck was on his side and the war ended within a few days. So Addison headed west to seek his fortune with the blood stained CS issued officer's coat and side arm, confident of his gambling skill but most of all his luck.

The Prize
Catherine Medovich 1849-1924

The mid nineteenth saw a mass migration to the Americas. The Medovichs were heading for Argentina when their ship was diverted to New York due to a major tropical storm in the south Atlantic. Medovich's home country was Austria. The Austria of the Austrian Hungarian Empire, which at the time included the Croatia peninsula. Music had always been part of their life and Catherine had been taught to play the violin and piano but her real talent was singing. Children performers were in demand and the Medovichs soon discovered that Catherine could earn a fair income by performing on the stage.

The civil war was raging at this time and New York was in the midst of civil strife with anti war protests turning into major riots. The Medovichs decided to seek their fortune out west. The transcontinental railway was newly completed and getting to California was only a matter of a few days travel. On the train they met the new owner of the Opera House in Virginia City and accepted an offer to perform there. Catherine was fourteen and more a young lady then a child. The offer was for her to perform solo, dressed as a European aristocrat with all the latest fashion from Paris. Catherine was a natural in that role with fair skin, brunette hair, deep dark brown eyes, and a soft sweet voice with a German accent. It was a class act and the city fell in love with her.

Virginia City, in1863 was the most important settlement between Denver and San Francisco. Gold was discovered in 1859 at the mouth of the six mile canyon near present day Virginia City. But it was the rich silver deposits, so-called Comstock Load, that made the city. Virginia City was a boisterous city with something going on 24 hours a day both above and below ground. There were nearly 30,000 residents. There were visiting celebrities, an opera house, opium dens, newspapers, competing fire companies, at least five police precincts, and a thriving red-light district. The International Hotel was a modern six stories hotel which boasted the first west of the Mississippi elevator, called a "rising room".

By the New Year, 1866 performance, Catherine was a veteran performer and a celebrity in Virginia City. Jack thought that she would be a perfect match for him, an asset to his status as an up and coming businessman and possible political career. He'd been courting her for the past year with negligible results. While Jack had matured in many aspects, he had little understanding of women, especially regarding wooing them. He had always been successful with women in the past and that was part of his problem. He was a good looking man and with his new status, he thought that any woman in their right mind would be glad to be with him. Jack have never pursued the opposite sex, they had always pursued him. What he did not realize was first the female needs to be interested. If she is not, then you must wait until she becomes interested. He needed to gain her respect, demonstrate his asset in a non intrusive manner. If successful she would show it in subtle body language and eye contact. It seemed the harder Jack tried the more distant she became.

The Antagonist

Without intent, Jack had developed a nemesis in a handsome ex confederate officer named Addison. This young man did not have Jack status but seemed to be beating Jack on all fronts.

He was an exceptional gambler; he'd won a number of pots from Jack. Jack did not depend upon gambling for a livelihood and could easily afford the lost but it did hurt his pride. Addison also seemed to have the inside track regarding Catherine's affections. She seemed so interested in his exploits as a confederate officer and his battle stories. Above all else, she seemed to be intoxicated by his smooth and natural grace. To top it off, he was going to escort her to the McKay's celebration after her New Year's performance.

Now Jack, as was the custom among fashionably dressed men of this day, carried a small derringer in his vest pocket. It had a gold chain attached to it that hung across the vest, similar to a watch chain. It was more for show than substance. If he really thought he needed a gun he'd choose a more lethal weapon, perhaps one of these new colt revolvers.

Addison was aware of Jack's growing dislike for him but he really did not take it seriously. After all he knew that Catherine was more interested in being with him than seeing him. Nothing of any consequence had occurred between them, only the goodnight embrace and kiss on the cheek. But he thoroughly enjoyed the prestige of her company. Addison did not appreciate music though and did not typically attend her shows.

He planned to have a few drinks at Delta Saloon, and then join her backstage after the New Year show. Catherine had had many suitors who would if possible marry her, put her in a gilded cage and display her as a trophy. The truth be known, she wanted none of that. She'd seen so many women used and abused just because they were wives.

She relished the role of a European aristocratic woman and thoroughly enjoyed her freedom.

There were very few places on earth like America where young women like Catherine were allowed to exercise her right to be free. While she did not want a serious suitor she did enjoy being in the company of men of substance and being escorted about town

Unintended Consequence

Jack was to meet David at the Delta Saloon to discuss the purchase of some Halet and Norcross stock. It looked promising and they would do well if they moved quickly. He'd had a few drinks and was still irked about the McKay's celebration. He'd thought that Catherine would come around and accompany him to the party. After all he was a man of substance while Addison was only a two bit gambler that has fought on the losing side.

When Jack saw Addison standing at the bar laughing and joking. Something swelled up inside him, a desire to kill him. He fought it off and looked toward David who was standing at the bar a short distance from Addison. But them Addison glanced up and as their eyes met he made a remark. Jack was standing no more than ten feet from him. Addison with a smirk on his face turned toward Jack exposing his side arm.

Jack reacted by pulling out his derringer and firing two shots directly at Addison. It is not so easy to hit your target under extreme tension at any distance with a short, barreled derringer. Jack missed him all together, shattering a bottle of whiskey on the bar just to the left of Addison, spattering whiskey and glass all over the nearby customers, slightly wounding a bystander to Addison's right. As the bar customer scattered for cover, Addison slowly pulled the CS sidearm from under his jacket and leveled it at Jack. Jack was fortunate that the CS pistol required cocking before it could be discharged which gave David enough time to grab Addison arm with his left hand, pushing it down towards the floor just as the gun discharged sending a built in to the hardwood, spattering wood pieces about. With almost the same motion he pulled out his knife and with his right hand thrust the six-inch blade through Addison's rib cage and into his lung.

Addison twitched for a moment, collapsed to his knee, and then fell forward onto the whiskey and glass cover floor, shortly drowning in his own blood.

Jack's Exodus 1866

For a period of time the bar customers were stunned and hesitated, giving David sufficient time to escape to the street. From the prospective of the bar customers, Jack and David have killed Addison in cold blood and they might have even planned his murder. The crowd quickly organized themselves and took to the pursuing of David. With the crowd preoccupied with David, Jack was able to slip away into the night. The mob caught up to David near Roberson's livery station, and after severely beating him, hung him from the hay lift. They left him hanging there and turned their attention to Jack but by this time Jack was nowhere to be found.

Jack had hid under the side porch of the Stanton's house on A Street until the mob grew tired of looking for him and headed to the Silver Dollar saloon, after all they would not enjoy their whiskey at the Delta with the pool of blood on the floor and Addison cold dead in it. And to be sure they intended to revel in and exaggerate their exploitation of the night.

When the coast was clear, Jack went looking for David. He found him quite dead and still hanging from the hay lift. He could do nothing now except save his own skin. He headed north east toward Louise Town, a small town about a mile from Virginia City. It was more like a miner's camp then a town but Jack was able to secure shelter from the night and the cold January weather. The next morning he hitched a ride with a teamster on route to Reno Meadows, about twenty mile to the north, where there was a railway stop. Jack knew that his life was in danger and he needed to get clear of Virginia City, the farther the better. He bought a ticket on the Southern Pacific for San Francisco and wired Western Union money gram to a mortician in Louis Town with instruction to cut down David and bury him with a stone headstone engraved, "David You Will Be Missed".

Sarah's Journey Home:

Nights in San Francisco can be quite cold, especially near the waterfront, any time of the year, but in December with the northern winds carrying freezing cold Sierra mountain air, blowing through the China Town's narrow alleys, it can be down right cold and so it was as Sarah laid on an old rice mat in the hospital. The hospital was located in a basement at the end of Cooper's alley in China Town. She was one of a dozen or so unwanted gravely sick women dying or already dead that night. In the morning, a watchman and a priest would make their rounds. The watchman would probe the patients to see if they were dead and the priest would give the last rights to everyone, dead or alive. Sarah's life was being choked out of her lungs by consumption but her will to live had died a long time ago. Sleepless nights can seem like an eternity but not this night, as Sarah slipped in and out of consciousness it was quickly fading into morning. As the sun's early morning rays penetrated the narrow alley, warmth began to fill her body and her thoughts drifted back to the night she met Jack. She had been sitting on the corner of Chartres and Ursuline in New Orleans, alone, cold and confused when Jack stopped and asked if she needed any help. He was so handsome and well dressed. He seen so considerate, kind and thoughtful. But she could not understand how he'd changed when she told him she was carrying his child. But no matter what, she could not help to still being in love with him.

And then she thought she heard a man's voice. It was in French, it was soft and reassuring. It was the German man from the ship. She remember him asking her if she needed a place to say. She'd stayed three months in a room above the Tavern.

He arrange for a Chinese midwife to assist in the birth and care of the child. She did not know why he was so kind but she knew that he wanted her to say. But she had one thing on her mind, Jack. As soon as she was able to, she began searching for him. She would start in the morning, looking about town, questioning Jack's friends and associates until late at night. She could not fine a trace of him and as time passed she drifted into a life of prostitution. She did not need the money, Nickelas would provide for her, perhaps it was love she was looking for. Or perhaps it was guilt, guilt for not loving and caring for their child, that she was running from. Or perhaps she was trying to hurt Jack by deserting their child so she moved to prostitution row, Waverly Place, just above Plymouth Square, submitting her body to anyone that would pay and her mind to opium.

Her thoughts drifted off to Effie, the madam of Waverly Place. She had been nice to her, they had a sexual relationship but Effie wanted more, love and stronger ties, closer relationship but Sarah could not, would not commit, for in truth without Jack there was no love in her.

As morning sun's rays broke through the fog and warmth drifted down Cooper's alley, Sarah could see the outline of a man standing in the doorway. He looked to be a young man and fine dressed. He walked down the row of bunks filled with the dead and dying. He held out his hand to her and smiled. At first Sarah hesitated but then she recognized him. He was her father, he looked just the way she remembered him all those years ago.

Still handsome with those smiling warm eyes. As she reached out to touch his hand, he said "Sarah it's time to come home".

Day 8 Afternoon unexpected visit

*I*was just fixing to leave, maybe have a late lunch at Jazz Club on Broadway when the phone rang. " Yes," I mumbled on the phone.

"This is Bemjamond Brovana and I wanted to ask if I could visit and take a closer look at the Las Arras" was the reply.

"The what and who?" I asked.

"I'am a coin collector that inquired about the thirteen coins, Bemjamond Brovana". He replied and added "I want to get more information and take some photos of the coins and the box. I want to forward them to the interested party".

"Who's the interested party?" I asked?

"I can only tell you that they are a very prominent old money European family" he said.

"The family that gave the Las Arras as a dowry?" I asked.

"Perhaps", was the reply.

"So I am going out for lunch and will be gone for a couple of hours. How about 5 PM" I suggested.

"That will work" was the reply.

When I was a boy, Broadway was just a street that paralleled Pacific Avenue.

Pacific was the last of the old Barbary Coast. It still had strip clubs and barkers. Pacific Street from Montgomery Street towards Kearney Street had metal arches across it. I remember the arch at Columbus Street that read "International Settlement."

I had a rather long lunch, good Italian food, a couple of drinks and some quality jazz, and when I returned to the Tavern that afternoon found the front door unlocked. I could not remember if I'd locked it or not, got mad at myself for not locking it and proceeded to discover someone had been messing around the bar area. Just about that time someone was knocking on the door.

"Hello Bemjamond Brovana, have you been waiting long?" I asked.

"No, I just arrived, parking is tough, it took some time to find parking." He said not looking at me.

"I have a feeling someone made an unauthorized visit while I was gone, any idea who that might be"? I asked sarcastically.

"It was not me, really I just arrived but I may not be the only person interested in the Las Arras. Perhaps your unauthorized visitor intended to make an unauthorized procurement of the Las Arras. Let's take a look at your fancy box and if it's the one, I strongly suggest you take my offer and be rid of it." He replied with eye contact and slightly cocked head.

I replied, "I'll keep that in mind." He didn't respond but I took a quick look down Grant street to be sure he was alone. I have no idea why, perhaps to change the direction of the conversation, I said "Do you know Grant Street was DuPont Street back in the day?".

He understood my intent, and said, "I will be waiting for your answer but my customer will not wait indefinitely" Turned and walked away.

Good old days

Chapter 8
The Tavern 1874

From Wagner's Beer Tavern, Fredric carried four pints of cool beer in a canvas bag slung over his shoulder. He delivered the beer for his father and made a little money for himself. He was heading for the road crew working on the Montgomery street extension. The extension followed the old Spanish military road that led to the Presidio. The road had been used continually despite the fact that it ran diagonal to the street grid laid out by Jasper O'Farrell, thirty years earlier. It had been the best year around route between the Northern dock area and the downtown area. Nickelas and his partner's, the Norwegian, brewery business had done well and when the Norwegian sold out to him and headed for gold country in 61, Nickelas moved the business to a building on DuPont Street. The building had been a dry goods store. He remodeled it, changed the interior to accommodate a bar and the front to look like a tavern. He started selling his beer by the glass.

He called it Wagner's Beer Tavern but everyone else just called The Tavern. His business had thrived largely due to his experience in the family's tavern in France. He introduced an evening spread to induce workmen getting off work to stop by. He only charged 5 cents a plate or all you can eat for 25 cents. It always included something hot like stew as well as bread and cheese. Unlike many drinking establishments of the period, uncivilized behavior was not tolerated. Nickelas was quite capable of enforcing order.

The extension project was scheduled to be finished by late 73 but had dragged out to September 74. Fredric had been able to make some extra money by delivering cold beer to the road crews at lunchtime but that was about to end. He was old enough now though to help his dad behind the bar. Originally his dad had brewed beer in the shed just behind the building but with inexpensive beer and other alcohols being available now, he just sold ready made beer and alcohol. The truth be told, his dad always sold more whiskey than beer. Fredric knew Nickelas was not his real father, but he was a fine dad and the only one he'd ever known. Nickelas cared for him since birth, having him baptized "Fredric Jack Wagner".

He supposed that was the same as adopting him. Fredric was his uncle's name. The name Jack was a mystery to him but he thought it might be his real father's name. Tucked away in a chest, Fredric had found an old leather handbag. It seemed quite well made with pearl handles and all. Nickelas told him that it was his mother's.

There were letters, receipts and a small box that contained coins. He did not know if the coins were worth anything because they were different then anything he'd seen in the bar.

There were names on the receipt, Sarah Montgomery and Jack Erskine. It seemed quite a coincidence that Sarah had the same last name as the Street just down the block. The receipts were from New Orleans and he thought Sarah and Jack might be related or even his parents. He'd imagine them as south aristocrats and that his father had been an officer in the confederate army and gave his life for a noble cause.

Elmo De Porto the Junkman

Fredric hurriedly finished sacking the empty bottles from behind the bar. He could hear the song of the junkman,"rags bottles sacks", in his heavy Tuscan accent. That was Elmo De Porto who collects junk for a living. Well that's how he got started anyway. Elmo was born on the Island of d Elbo, in the Ligurian Sea just off the coast of the Duchiesthe of Tuscany. No one knew the date for sure but he said about 1843.

He was illiterate in both Tuscano and English but real smart about everything else. Elmo had come to San Francisco in the early 60s as a cabin boy aboard the Italian schooner, Elisabeth.

After seeing San Francisco, he decided that this would be his home. He did odd jobs about the waterfront and earned enough to buy a well-used Studebaker Overland Prairie Schooner and converted it to a hauling wagon. He had to swap out the oxen rig for a single horse setup, take off the canvas top and enlarge the bed. He purchased an old Wells Fargo stage Tennessee Mule and he was in the freight business.

Because of racial attitudes at the time, he found it difficult to get the conventional freight business but he discovered that it was acceptable to be in the garbage and junk business.

He worked long hours and saved his money. After the stock market crash of 77, some of the biggest landowners in the city were forced to sell land. Elmo purchased some vacant land on the steep side of telegraph hill. He purchased and placed a surplus prefab house on the property. These prefabs houses that were built in China, shipped to and assembled. Throughout San Francisco they were being replaced by grander structures and often sold dirt cheap just to get them removed. He sent for this second cousin, Victoria, married her and started a family. He bought chickens and goats and with her help started a small farm selling eggs, goat milk and goat cheese to the newly arrived Italian families.

Friends for Life

Giovanni was Elmo's third of ten children and Fredric's best friend. They both attended St Ignatius's Catholic primary school. They first met one day while Fredric and Maria Qui, his sister, were walking to school. The three McDonald brothers were harassing them as usual. They were calling him a chink lover and his sister a half breed chink. The oldest brother, older and bigger then Fredric, would grab and pull Maria Qui braid to force Fredric to retaliate. Then the three brothers would jump him, punching, kicking and knocking him to the ground. Giovanni who had witnessed this same endeavor some time could not tolerate it any longer and that day jumped in to help Fredric.

Now Giovanni was a junkman's son and tough as they come. In short order he and Fredric had the three of them on the run. From that day on Fredric and Giovanni were the best of friends.

The Tavern was Elmo's, the junk man, last stop of the day and from there he took the Montgomery extension stopping at the junkyard to sell the goods, then he'd take the old Presidio road, past the Washerwoman Lagoon to the Miller's dairy where he stabled his mule.

Giovanni worked with his dad in the afternoon and helped unload the bags of empty beer bottles and junk from the wagon, Fredric liked to ride with them to the dairy. He and Giovanni would unhitch and attend to the mule, while Elmo stored the wagon. Elmo would always give them 5 cents each before heading home.

Fredric and Giovanni would stick around the dairy to see the twin sister, Rachael and Isabel. They were identical twins and it took awhile to be able to distinguish between them. Fredric and Giovanni knew them well enough to distinguish them from a distance.

When the girls had finished their chores, the four of them would wander down by the lagoon and watch the washerwomen finish the day's work, pack up the laundry, their children and head home. The girl had to be home early but there was always time to do the things girls and boys do. Then more often than not, Fredric and Giovanni would head for Pacific Street, the center of the Barbary Coast. To be young, in the Barbary Coast at night among the night people, barkers, gamblers, hustlers, working women, with 5 cents in your pocket is a freedom experienced by only a few.

Day 9 Bella Union

I was just returning from a clothes shopping trip, wanted to clean up my act. Why I want to lose my invisibility is confusing, after all I'd worked to create it. I'm not sure but it might be Gregoria. I noticed someone sitting on the steps in front of the Tavern. I was hoping that it was her. I assumed she was going to hassle me about the sale of the property. She was not dressed in her CEO outfit but a neat looking summer dress.

It was Indian summer in the city and the days were beautiful and warm. Her hair was shining in the sunlight and I realized my interest was more than business. "Hey baby are you going my way" I said in my best Bogy imitation.

She looked up and smiled as she recognized me and said "only if you are buying coffee" in her best Lauren Bacall imitation. I thought about replying as Bogy but figured it's a pretty poor imitation so instead in my normal voice" I'd love to".

"Is your coffee machine behind the bar working? I like to visit with you and I like privacy". She said.

My coffee was bad so we opened a bottle of wine. Her white summer dress, the kind the girls in WW2 wore, gave me the feeling it could be 1943 again. We talked about everything except the sale. The conversation got around to the history of the North Beach area, in particular Bella Union, a saloon in the old Barbary Coast.

unreturned love is almost love

Chapter 9
The Madam

The old Barbary Coast

The Barbary Coast had a long history, over 70 years, in San Francisco. Its origin was in the tents and board shanties in the vicinity of Clark's Point, about where Broadway and Pacific streets run into the Bay. A local news paper described the Barbary Coast as the haunt of the low and the vile of every kind. It was a rather dangerous place in the 1850s but after a few hangings and increased pressure from civic groups it became somewhat safer. It was said that by the late 1860s, San Francisco possessed a red-light district larger than those of many cities several times its size. At that time the Barbary Coast began on Pacific near Montgomery and followed it through to Stockton, with various channels leading into it from Kearney and DuPont Streets. Fredric and Giovanni were well known among many of the patrons and operators of the establishments, Dance Halls, Concert Saloons and Melodeons. Some of the places only have piano, others would have more instruments like fiddles and brass horns, but the music would drift out into the street and blend with the people to create a symphony. Inside the Dance Halls men and harlots stood side by side at the bar, usually to one side of the room with the musicians on the other side and men and women dancing in the middle. Most of the halls were cellars with low slung ceilings.

French demi-monde Effie Gregory 1843- 1899

But the Bella Union was different, above ground in a high ceiling building. The interior has French decor with chandeliers and red printed wallpaper. The owner, Effie was an ex-madam, originally from Marseilles. She came to San Francisco in 1857, one of the "French demi- monde, carefully chosen from the bagnios of Paris and Marseilles for their beauty, amiability, and skill". Effie was a young fine-looking prostitute with long legs, bright blue eyes, long shiny auburn hair and a charming smile and she was looking for a better life. She was all that but also smarter than the average hooker. She quickly elevated herself to a madam status and operated a high-class house for a number of years on Waverly Place, the prostitute row just above Portsmouth Squared that serviced the white community.

Effie was not French even though she spoke France as if it's her first language. She was mostly Scottish. Her father, a renowned musician, had relocated with his daughter, her governess and his mistress to Marseilles for the weather and employment opportunities, leaving her mother in Edinburgh. They had settled in a small town, Cassis, just south of Marseilles. He and his mistress would be gone for months on end. She and the governess were left to their own devices.

When she was thirteen her father returned unexpectedly to find her and the Governess involved in sexual diversions; he brandished her from the house. His puritan ethics could not condone such behavior. He was ashamed of her and besides he had some sexual aspirations for the governess himself .

She had little options except to move to Marseilles and start working as a prostitute. Perhaps she had other options but his one suited her fine. She might well have spent her life there except for the enterprising Yankees in San Francisco. She heard on the street that there was an opportunity to move to America and be paid handsomely.

Like many prostitutes, Effie's sexual relationship with men was strictly business. For love and companionship, she preferred women, other prostitutes like herself. Over the years that she was a prostitute and a madam, she had a number of sexual liaisons. But one stood out.

She was a beautiful young woman from New Orleans. She'd had a relationship with a man that produced a child. She could not seem to or want to forget him. Effie always felt his present between them, even while making love. It seemed to Effie that Sarah only sought a temporary solace through sex, much like Effie male customers. Effie truly loved her but tried as she might Sarah would not or could not return the love.

Sarah's mental and physical condition began to deteriorate. She used ever increasing amounts of opium and was in more or less a constant state of opium induced stupor. Her condition decayed to the point where she could no longer work. It seemed that Sarah did not want to live without her man. Effie heard that she had been taken to Cooper Ally to die. Effie hoped that she might be able to rescue her but it was too late. Effie requests that Sarah not be buried in the Sailor's cemetery with so many unknown, unwanted souls. Effie paid to have her buried in the new cemetery at Lone Mountain. She ordered a beautiful marble statue of a weeping child with the inscription" I hope you find in death that which you could not find in life". Effie did not know exactly why she chose a child, perhaps she thought about Sarah's motherless child.

Effie could still feel the pain of being torn away from her mother years ago. When the sight of Sarah and so many other young women wasting away became too much to bear, Effie switched careers. She opened the Bella Union as a stylish Concert Saloon and catered to upper crest. Dancing was not allowed and no fraternizing with the employees. Her doorman's job, unlike the usual barker, was not to entice people into her establishment but to screen out the riff raff. No unescorted female, no trouble makers, only well dressed, well-mannered customers were permitted in. She'd often stand near the front door so she could greet the customers and if necessary reject the ones that slipped by the screening.

She was always amused and sometimes abased by the multitude of petty thieves, house burglars, tramps, whoremongers, lewd women, cutthroats, and what all that paraded past on the street. Many of them were so young, just boys and girls. she assumed that they, like her, had been abandoned and left to life's fate. There were always a number of local young men hanging around, just to get a peek at this lewd but terribly interesting world inside the Bella Union. If they stay too long, she'd have the doorman dispersed them. There was one young man though that had something so familiar about him. She was told that he was the son of the Tavern owner, up on DuPont street. It was his eyes and nose that seemed to ring a bell. Then out of the blue it came, Sarah. Yes that was it, he looked as if he could be related to her. She knew the Tavern's owner, Nickelas and he sure didn't look like his son.

Effie 's Epiphany1876

Effie had observed Fredric a number of times over the past year or so, some time peering through the gold leaf trimmed windows and other time just strolling past on Pacific Street, some time by himself and other times with his buddy. One misty cold evening while greeting customers, she noticed Fredric peering through the window. She instructed the doorman to bring him to her office via the side door. The office was quite large with all the comfort of a fine hotel. It had imported rugs on the floors, French drapes on the windows, fine setting chairs, an oversized day-bed and, of course, a big official looking desk.

She gave him a glass of bourbon to ward off the night's chill. A fifteen year old son of a tavern owner would be quite familiar with hard spirits and there was nothing out of place regarding this. She herself did not touch alcohol of any kind. As they talked, more like she questioned him regarding his background, she became convinced that he was Sarah's son.

His mannerisms, the way he looked past you until he responded and them he looked through you. His smile, which was reflected as much in his eyes as in his lips, was grand. Suddenly she felt an urge to kiss him, she tried to dismiss it through logic, he was just a boy, I'm old enough to be his mother, to no avail. This was an unusual emotion for her, to be attracted to a male, perhaps it was reflection of her longing for Sarah. For a woman of worldly experience, both sexually and socially, this did not make any sense.

But be that what it may, there was no turning back now. She found herself seducing him with prolonged eye contact and soft touches. He responded with youthful urgency but to her surprise some capability. She had not had any sex for some time and she found the intercourse quite enjoyable. Enjoyable but rather short, as he came to fruition with a sudden thrust and she unexpectedly had an orgasm. It had been a number of years since she had an orgasm and the first time with a male.

As the intense pleasure of the orgasm subsided she was overwhelmed by a feeling of remorse, remorse not for the sexual act but something else. If only things had been different all those years ago, perhaps she could have met her man and they might have been one of the lucky few. The ones that live, love, have children, grandchildren and grow old together. She asked him to leave and said that she would not see him again. She instructed the doormen that in the future not to allow him in the Bella Union. She returned to her office and sat at her desk for a while but the feeling of remorse would not abate, She screamed "Dam you father" and began to cry.

Day 10 Cleaning up

*T*he abandoned forsaken feeling of the Tavern's interior was getting to me so I decided even if it did not matter I was going to straighten the area. I began sweeping, straightening up the table and chair.

I opened the front doors to let in some fresh air and rediscovered how fresh the early fall morning San Francisco air could be. A slight northern breeze off the Pacific ocean had cleared the morning fog and the sun's rays were high lighting the downtown skyscrapers. I glanced up Grant Street and observed the want-to- be CEO lady was across the street. She noticed me and waved with a warm smile.

"Hello Johnny, how are you on this fine fall day"? She asked. Wow, I thought "It's been a long time since I had heard Johnny and even longer since it sounded so good."

"Where did you get Johnny" I asked?

"Do you like it?, my grandmother said they always called you Johnny. Did you know that your great grandfather Fredric had been shanghaied and spent a number of years at sea. I have a lot to do this morning but I was hoping to get together this afternoon. Will that work"?

Chapter 10
The La Ninfa

Mr. Nelson

The La Ninfa, a schooner out of Plymouth, England was on her third year of a four year whaling exposition. Her Captain, Mr. Nelson, an ex British Navy officer, had for financial reasons become a whaler a dozen years ago. Mr. Nelson's only naval distinction was that he was, although it being quite distant, a relative of Lord Nelson, the hero of Trafalgar. His great aunt, Jennifer, always remarked when he was a child about his resemblance to the Horatio, she always referred to Lord Nelson as Horatio. As the Captain matured though, he noted that almost everybody had a famous somebody somewhere in their bloodline. He did his best to conceal or ignore it. The Captain's father's surname, his real surname was Harrington. He was a first cousin to the Lord. The Captain had tried to forget that and his father too but the whole affair was like a blood stain on your shirt, it would not fade.

In the early nineteen century, a man's home was his castle and a castle was his home. Mr. Harrington had an alcohol problem and a habit of sleeping with his daughters, and his wife had a habit of ignoring it. The Captain was an accident. Neither his mother nor his father planned his conception. But then his mother was this sister. He and his sister, mother left England for rural Ireland for his great aunt's home and his birth. His great aunt welcomed him into this world and gave him shelter and love. His poor sister, his mother returned to England to live with her sister and mother. The Captain never saw her again; she was so ashamed of her father's betrayal that she could not bring herself to confront it or her son. She tolerated, endured and withered on the vine. She could not entertain the thought of a male companionship. The youngest sister found a female companion; which was acceptable in Victorian England. The other sisters became old maids together.

Immaculate Conception

It was years after his birth that he learned that his mother was his sister but not because his aunt fibbed to him but because she only told him as much as he could handle. She was always aunty, never mother. Jennifer knew that lies were like weeds, one always results in many more in your garden. So she always told the truth, but never more than necessary. When he was eight or so he insisted on knowing who his mother was. Jennifer told him the story of a neighbor of the Virgin Mary, the mother of god. It happened that her neighbor became pregnant by her fiancé, a young man from her tribe. But he had an accident and was killed. The punishment at that time for conceiving without being married was death by stoning. She did not tell her parents but her mother was rather observant and suggested that perhaps there might be another Immaculate Conception. In those days, immaculate conceptions were not all that unusual. When the young lady found a new suitor, married and lived happily ever after, her parents raised the child as if it was their child.

To tell the truth, that story did not satisfy him but rather it confused him. And when he asked about his father, she told him the story about Jesus, the son of god whose father was god. He then wanted to know if he was a god because of all that talk about immaculate conceptions. His aunt told him that many people believe that man is made in the image of god but she thought that he looked more like Lord Nelson. Over the years the whole truth was revealed to him, that it was not immaculate conception, but by then he understood that conception does not define a man. That his aunt had given him a foundation as good as any man could expect and a great surname.

He often thought about his mother, his sisters and only hoped they would also find the love he'd found with Jennifer. His aunt, Jennifer Nelson, had a clear head and vast experience. She rescued him from a life of depravity, educated and loved him. She once told him, "the truth" of life. Life is not an accident, yes evolution is how living things change but not how they started. You can not separate life from the other physical properties, such as gravity, it is part and partial of the universe. "Life is everywhere just like gravity in the universe". If there was a god, he'd deal with your father and set your sisters free.

When Mr. Nelson was thirteen, his aunt arranged for him to join the British Navy as a midshipman on HMS Black Prince, a 9250-ton ironclad frigate under the command of his third cousin. He worked and studied hard and by the time he was twenty eight he had his own command, a schooner the HMS Scorpion, a 2750-ton ironclad turret ship built at Birkenhead, England. She was one of two ships secretly ordered from the Laird shipyard by the Confederate government in 1862. The British government seized the pair of ironclads in October 1863 before they could be delivered.

Scorpion was assigned to the Channel Fleet until 1869, with time out for a refit that reduced her sailing rig from a bark to a schooner. In late 1869, the ironclad was sent to Bermuda for coast and harbor defense service. Mr. Nelson joined her there and took command.

Whaling Business

He'd married Martha Van Housing, the daughter and only offspring of a wealthy South African businessman. The Captain was looking forward to a life of leisure but when the gold crash of 71 had all but eliminated this, Mr. Nelson resigned his commission and sought to build his wealth as a businessman. Thus he entered into the commercial whaling business.

Mr. Nelson's connection and a thousand pound sterling he was able to purchase the La Ninfa, a 2600 ton wood hull schooner. She was refitted for the whaling trade. Although she was out dated, she was still a solid well maintained vessel and a fine buy. With Mr. Nelson's sea experience and family connection he had little trouble recruiting investors. He and his associates would finance these whaling expositions by selling shares in London and other major cities in England. Whaling ventures were rather risky business but Nelson had made a reasonable return for his investors in the last two expositions. He hoped this would be his last, that it would be profitable enough to return to England, sell the La Ninfa, retire and open a haberdashery in the midlands.

Perhaps the haberdashery was really more his wife's idea then his. He rather enjoyed the adventure of whaling. In many ways he was pleased regarding this change in fortune and thought that he was better suited for the life of a whaler than as a British naval officer. His wife, Martha saw the turn of events as a disaster. She'd been raised to be the wife of a gentleman, not rouge, a whaler. She had second thoughts about accompanying her husband on this voyage to say nothing of dragging their daughters along too. And her oldest daughter, Isla was not shy about registering her distaste regarding this voyage.

Isla had been continually complaining since they left England. For her, this voyage was more akin to exile and punishment. Punishment for having the wrong parents. Her greatest desire would be to return to their home, school and friends. They, her sister and her mother were delighted to hear that La Ninfa would lay over in San Francisco but disappointed beyond belief to hear no one except the Mr. Jones would go ashore. The captain feared, and rightly so, the losing of his crew, including his family, to the allure of San Francisco. So far this voyage has been rough and not every successful. He hoped to have more luck in the mid Pacific hunting ground. He needed to lie over in San Francisco bay to unload and market the whaling oil and baleen harvested thus far and replenish equipment, food and men.

Day 11 CEO becomes Gregoria

I was having a late morning coffee at Roma on Columbus St when my morning daydream, my big escape plans, were interrupted "Johnny I thought I might find you here. I stop by the Tavern to get your decision on the offer". She said. Hay what happen to "I'll see you this afternoon? and do you know a Bemjamond Brovana?" I asked.

"Oh it's a long story" she replied and without answering my question said, "are you interested in seeing where your GGGrandmother is buried? I've contacted the Lone Mountain Cemetery people and they gave me directions. Have you ever been there"? She asked.

"No I am not sure if I want to and no I never have" I answered.

For the first time I could see the veneer of youth give way to a mature woman. You could see the traces of time and stress on her pretty face. Ok maybe she is not a spring chicken but she is still an attractive woman.

"Oh come on, it's a nice day, the cemetery is on Masonic." she replied glaring at me and then perceiving my thoughts added, "yes I've also been around the block".

It turned out to be a nice day, the sun had worked its way through the fog and there was a soft breeze from the ocean. She'd brought a lunch and blanket. As we sat near a marble statue of a weeping child, Gregoria began talking about being raised in North Beach. That like me, she had run away but waiting until after graduating from UC. She said "like a moth she was drawn to the hi finance world and a life glamour of New York". She continued "same old story: husband, infidelity, disappointment and return to mother".

Her family went way back to the early days of the city. Her Grandmother would tell her stories of the area and people. One of the names Gregoria recalled was the Tavern owner Chris David. She said she had some business to attend to and would drop me off at the Tavern. On the drive back I invited her back to the Tavern for drinks that evening.

Chapter 11
Chris David 1879

New Owner 1879

By the end of the 70's San Francisco had changed from a gold rush to an industrial and finance economy. The center of the whaling activities had shifted from New Bedford to San Francisco and the city built an industry around it. The Tavern had also changed. It had a new owner, Chris David and a new type of customer. No one seemed to know much about Chris except that was not his real name. Rumors had it that he'd had some kind of scrape in Virginia City before moving to the City.

The majority of the Tavern's customers were now tradesmen associated with the Whaling business. Many of them had moved from the East following that business. They were sailors and the men that supplied equipment and maintained. And when necessary provided some of the replacement crew.

Nickelas had moved to Hawaii with his wife and daughter. He found the racial intolerance towards Yan and their daughter was unbearable. The riots of 1875 fueled by anti-Chinese furor were the final blow. He'd heard that the Hawaii Islands was quite racially diverse and culturally tolerant. He'd left his 17 year old son in San Francisco to finish high school and agreed to have him work with the new owner in exchange for bread and board. Nickelas expected his son to join him in a few months but it would be many years and seem more like another lifetime before they'd meet again.

Times were changing, gone was the public safety committees, the Pickhandle Brigade, composed of citizens equipped with sawed off pick handles, to maintain order and serve out justice. The city had an official police force, not that effective but enough to give it the appearance of legitimacy. The Barbary Coast had moved up the hill and now fully engulfed the Tavern. Chris Davidson, the new owner, had a different business philosophy than Nickelas, to make money any way he can. harlots, gamblers, whalers and shanghais were freely mingling in the Tavern.

If prostitution is the oldest profession in the world then gambling and crimping (shanghaiing) are tied for second. Crimping is really a form of slavery. Men, women and children throughout history have been forced to labor for prolonged periods against their will.

Shanghaiing, just as prostitution and gambling were sanctioned throughout the city's establishment. Without the passive approval of the police and political bosses, what was in effect the kidnapping and enslavement of working men could not exist. Not only did some of the city's police and politicians look the other way but some were actively involved.

There was a whole spectrum of businesses, boarding houses, saloons, dance halls, bordellos, and the Whitehalls (small swift sailing boats) that were all part of the culture and practice of shanghaiing. Crimper delivered bodies, not always able bodied, for pay. They did not discriminate, any man, woman or child over twelve were potential victims. It was reported that even the sick and dying, sometimes already dead, were delivered. Chris and the Tavern were just one of the elements of that business. The Tavern had become fertile ground for the recruiting of not so willing men to crew the whaling fleet. Chris was getting his share, two months share of the recruits advance pay and to Chris it was just business.

Uncle Thomas

It was late in the afternoon and Fredric was cleaning up around the bar, sweeping the floors, emptying the spittoons and so on. Chris and Alfaro, Giovanni's oldest brother, were behind the bar. It was still early and there were only a few customers, the real lost souls that dependent upon the booze to relieve the pain of life. One of the customers, a rough looking older man who definitely needs a bath and a change of clothes, said "I know you". The man was not looking at Fredric but directly at Chris.

Chris glanced at the man for a moment and slowly moved towards the other end of the bar; he said something to Alfredo and disappeared into the storeroom. Alfredo came out from behind the bar and told the man to fine another place to drink and with more force than necessary escorted him toward the door. The man spun away and shouted "you're Gilchrist Fergus Erskine, Jack I'm your brother. Don't you remember me"? Everything seemed to stop for a moment, Alfredo took a step backward, and Chris came from out of the storeroom and said "yes, how are you Thomas, you look so much like dad". He motioned to Alfredo to get him out as he said "Thomas I'll meet you outside".

Gilchrist Fergus Erskine, Jack! Fredric knew that name, Jack Erskine, but he couldn't place it. Yes the receipts in the old handbag. Fredric turned abruptly and ran up the stairs to his room and found the handbag his father Nickelas had left in his keep. Nickelas had said "someday you'll prize his bag, keep it safe". Fredric had not looked inside it for some time but he remembered wondering about the names and who they could be. Could they be related to him? He knew Sarah was his real mother's name. Inside were the receipts, a small box containing thirteen silver coins and some other stuff. Fredric carefully unfolded the receipts and read the names, Sarah Monogamy, Jack Erskine, David Mc Lish, the dates, 1857 and the place, New Orleans. It was a receipt for passage, paid in advance, to San Francisco. Could it be, was Jack Erskine his real father? Sarah Montgomery his mother? And who was this David Mc Lish? Chris Davidson, Gilchrist, David, Chris Davidson!

Resentment boiled up inside him, he stormed down stairs and confronted Chris just as he was taking off his work smock. Chris was startled by Fredric 's posture, demure and facial expressions. There were tears streaming down Fredric's face. Chris looked at the Handbag Fredric held and recognized it as Sarah's. Fredric was staring deeply into Chris' eyes. At that moment Chris, Jack, Gilchrist Fergus Erskine, realized that Fredric was his son. Fredric asked" where is my mother? What did you do to her? You bustard"! Fredric flung himself, arms flying towards Chris. Alfredo grabbed him and wrapped him in his arm and held him tightly until Fredric relaxed and then released him. Fredric dropped the handbag, turned and ran out the door and almost knocked Thomas, Chris brother, to the ground. Fredric hesitated for a moment, just long enough to stabilize Thomas. As Fredric started down the DuPont Street he heard Thomas ask" Young man, do I know you?"

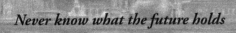

Chapter 12
Fredric's Voyage 1877

Shanghaied

Fredric, still dazed and overwhelmed by the fact that Chris was his biological father, walked down DuPont street, turned on to Broadway and headed towards the Bella Union, he was not sure of why, he just instinctively felt that Effie knew his mother. As usual, the doormen at the Bella Union would not let him in or pass a note to Effie. As he stood outside the Bella Union pondering the day's events, he could feel someone too near to him, he could even smell him. It was Thomas, he must have followed me, Fredric thought.

Fredric turned to tell him to get lost but before he could say a word he felt a heavy blow across his shoulders, and then a gunny sock like material pulled tightly about his mouth and eyes. Then a vary strong man dragged, lifted him and tossed him into a waiting wagon. He could feel and smell the present of Thomas next to him as the wagon rattled down the cobblestone street. The wagon stopped and he was roughly pulled from the wagon and heaved in a boat. Fredric knew enough to realize that he was being shanghaied and that the boat was a one of the Whitehall, the small crafts used to transport goods to waiting ships. Fredric began to struggle, kicking, screaming to no avail. The men punched him and told him to quiet down but when he persisted he received a blow to the head that knocked him unconscious.

Throughout history and up to the early twentieth century, danger and risk were very much part of everyday life. Children would experience death and injury to their friends and family. Most of the adults of this time lived with damage and disfigured fingers, arms and legs as the result of daily life. Just handling livestock such as poorly trained horses was fraught with danger, but these dangers paled compared to the life of a whaler, possibly the most dangerous business of the time. As Fredric regained consciousness he found himself a part of this world. He was cold and numb with pain. It was dark, smelly and damp. He figured that he was in the hole of some ship.

An Old Man's Gift

Fredric was not only cold but also becoming seasick from the continuing pitching and pounding of La Ninfa as she headed to the open sea through the infamous potato patch, the tortured sea just outside the gate. In the darkness he could feel the present of another person and by his smell he knew that it was Thomas. He could hear him fighting for air and that wheezy sound old people made when they breathed.

Fredric wished he was anywhere else except here, cold, damp and worst, next to his old man. Through the breathing and wheezing noise, Fredric could hear Thomas asking "are you Jack's son"? The last thing Fredric wanted to think about, but despite his discomfort, cold, damp, seasick, Fredric could hear himself replay "I do not know". "You have the Erskine's look, your head, your chin, your walk. I believe that I am your uncle" the old man replied. Uncle or not, Fredric did not want anything to do with this decrepit old man.

They laid there silent for a long period as the cold creped into their body and penetrated their bones. Driven by survival instincts, the need for warmth, and despite the smell, Fredric crawled close to Thomas. Thomas, who was wearing a thick wool coat, opened his coat and wrapped it around Fredric. Despite his loathing for this old man, Fredric welcomed the warmth. The old man began to tell him about Jack, their family and their life in West Virginia. How Jack had left without even a goodbye. How the years for toil could not coach a living from that section of land; that in the end, it killed his father and made his mother a young widow and drove her to her grave. He'd tried to keep the family together. But after burying the youngest child, his sister ran away with a drifter, and there was nothing left but to drift off himself. He'd drifted right into the Confederate army and had fought for the cause even those he was dead set against slavery. He told how the experience of war had killed the last vestige of belief in the god almighty. His only relief now came in a bottle. But now somehow life, destiny or something, had put them together.

Fredric was cold, seasick; he was hurting from the beating and the hard oak planks he was laying on and wished his old guy would shut up. Thomas fell silent for a while, Fredric thought he might have died but then Thomas said, "Son I saw my dad just now and he said I must give his grandson my coat. That I'm close to death and will soon be cold and not able to help warm you. He hopes that this will show you that life is benevolent, if not fair". Fredric tried to stop him with pleads that he needed it and not to die but to no avail. He said "Son, do not deny an old man's last chance to do some good". As Fredric put on the coat, Thomas straightened it up and pulled it up tight around his neck like father would do for his son. Then the old man laid back down; in a few moments his breathing began to soften, the wheezing stopped with a final grasp, the death rattle and he was gone.

Seaward Bound 1877

There is an old Irish saying, if the sea gets into a young man's blood, he'll be lost to her. And surely the Irish should know for they have lost so many to her.

Fredric awoke to the sound of the hatch opening and blinding light. He had no sense of how long he'd been in the dark. As he adjusted to the light he could see a seaman, short in stature with long stringy black hair tied back by a sweat stained red scarf. His weathered facial skin reflected many years spent at sea. He shouted in an authoritarian a British accent, "to ya feet mat, the captain has called for all hands top side". As Fredric started for the hatch opening, the seaman was probing Thomas. Fredric could hear him say, "going to be hell to pay! Captain has ordered all hands on deck. Word of advice mate, on a ship the captain tis law". Fredric crawled out of the hold and joined the crew on the deck. He was roughly moved about until he found a place near the end of a line of thirty or so tough men.

The Captain and three officers, who were quite well dressed and looking like British officers, were standing on the foredeck above them. The Captain asked about the new crew members. The black haired man with the red scarf stepped forward, pointed toward Fredric and replied, "only one man alive, the other died sir". The captain looked directly at Fredric as he spoke, "you mean this boy"? "Aye sir, other men are dead sir". At this point an older bald headed sailor spoke without stepping forward, "sir I was told they were both healthy able body seamen when they were delivered, sir." "How did the other man die"? The captain asked. "I do not know sir, but he looked mighty old sir" the bald headed sailor replied. Looking directly at the sailor, the captain said "Mr. Jones, you'll bring the deceased man top side and read him for disposal, do not want him to infect the crew. For your incompetence, your share of the profits will be reduced by one half the costs of these men and that does not account for the lost revenue due to the operating short handed." He turned and spoke to the officer on his right, "Mister Robert, prepare for a Christian burial, it is the least we can do for the poor soul. The captain knew in his heart that he was not truly a Christian. He felt that Christianity was just the latest mythology in a long line of mythologies starting long before the Athenian age. Not that the Captain was a faithless man. His faith was that life is benign. That no matter how depressed the situation seemed, the goal was to make the best of it. He was still awed by the miracle of birth and finality of death. But in those days, to act Christian was the wise thing to do.

Mr. Nelson, looking at the crew, asked, ``Who will speak for him?" "I will", Fredric replied.

The captain looked directly at him and said, "sailor you will address me, sir or Mr. Nelson". "Sir, Mr. Nelson, I will speak for him and can I help ready him" Fredric replied. "Sailor, did you know him well?" asked the Captain. "Yes sir, he was my uncle, Thomas Erskine, a truly fine man." The captain spoke "Mt Roberts, have the first mate look after this boy and see to it that he stays alive. We paid a lot of money for those two and I intend to make the best of a bad deal".

A Christen Burial

Mr. Jones and Fredric hauled Thomas topside. Mr. Jones began searching through Thomas's pockets for valuables and when Fredric protested, Mr. Jones grabbed him by the neck and told him to button up his lip or else and to never call him Mr. Jones, "tis for officers, just call me Jones".

Fredric was glad that Thomas had given him the warm wool coat before he died or else Jones was sure to claim it. The search only yielded a few silver coins and a small ivory Irish cross. Jones put them into a leather pouch fashioned by a belt about his waist; then ordered Fredric to wrap him in linen over his clothing. As Fredric wrapped the linen about Thomas, he could feel how thin and frail Thomas was and he thought about the years toiled on that section of land and how little it yielded. They then carried and placed him on a plank on the lee side railing.

Fredric stayed with him while Jones reported to the office of the deck. Fredric laid his hand on Thomas and said "I will not forget you and I will survive and make you and my grandfather proud".

With the crew, officers and the captain's family gathered about, the captain nodded wards Fredric and said "son would you speak for your uncle". Fredric began to say the Lord's Prayer in Latin "pater noster, qui es in caelis, sanctificetur nomen tuum. Adveniat regnum tuum. Fiat voluntas tua, sicut in caelo et in terra. Panem nostrum quotidianum da nobis hodie, et dimitte nobis debita nostra sicut et nos dimittimus debitoribus nostris. Et ne nos inducas in tentationem, sed libera nos a malo. Amen." as he was taught by father Ignacio. He then spoke in English "God this man has spent many years in hell, now it is time to take his soul to your house. He gave me his love and what little life he had left. I pray that I will be worthy of it". Fredric was not sure if he was a Christian or not.

He'd not given it much thought. But just in case all that religious stuff was true he wanted to send his uncle off in the best possible way. Only the Captain's oldest daughter had enough command of Latin to understand the prayer and was quite impressed with him. The captain understood just enough to know it was Latin and that Fredric was well educated. Without any hesitation the Captain continued with the burial, "To the sea we commit the body of Thomas Erskine, a righteous man, for safekeeping until on judgment day when the sea will give up his soul". It was a short and not the traditional farewell, the Captain had buried many a sailor, be Christian or not, and saw no need to be hypocritical at this point.

Sea Legs

Like most situations, with time you become accustomed to it and make the necessary adjustments and so within a few weeks Fredric got over being seasick, gained his sea legs and began to function as part of the crew. He was given some spare seaworthy clothes, boots, jack tar and such. He was assigned an empty hammock, probably belonging to an unfortunate sailor that was lost at sea. When not processing whales, his job would be to assist the carpenter in maintaining and repair of the ship. The La Ninfa had left San Francisco on a South Eastern course and had to pick up the trade winds that would carry her to the mid Pacific hunting ground. Life aboard the ship settled into a routine of long hours of boredom, performing work duties and standing watch. Twenty days out of port they'd seen a ship heading west and the scuttlebutt had it that they were laden with whale catch.

The crew of a nineteen century whaler consisted mainly of waterfront drifters. Unlike military crews of the nineteen century, the crews of the whalers were organized more like the pirate ships of the eighteenth century. The willing and able held positions of authority, this included the officers. The officers generally had formal training and often military experience. The men were accustomed to a violent lifestyle. Fredric soon found that life aboard was much like a dog fight and because he was young and new, he'd have to prove his worth, physically and mentally. For the most part the men were not cruel and some harassment was well meaning.

They saw Fredric as being in the same boat as them and to survive he needed to toughen up. Of course there were the ones who meant him harm and that was part of his education too, the ability to spot and deal with them.

Like most pecking orders, the toughest guy would be the last to worry about; it was the guys near the bottom that were set upon proving they could dominate you. Orrick, an American born Swede, was at the top of the order. He was six feet tall with a frame made of only bone and muscle. He was the harpoon man. He could throw a 15 pound harpoon and hit his mark from 50 feet. For some reason, be befriended Fredric and took it upon himself to tutor him. He could see that Jones had it in for Fredric and one evening while they were standing the dog watch, Orrick took him aside and told him to beware of Jones. He told him that there were no fair fights, only winner and loser, that Jones was ruthless and for sure would used his knife. He told him not to let Jones get close, if he could help it because Jones would butt head and try to bite off his ear. The ear thing was a status thing. He said Fredric must pick the time and the place to his advantage. Any dog can be beaten given a worthy opponent and the right strategy. If he gives Jones a good fight then others will take notice that they too could be had.

Mr. Jones

Fredric did not choose Jones as the adversary but Jones for some reason or another had decided that Fredric was to blame regarding the shanghai blander, that if Fredric was more competent the Captain might give him his full share of the profits. Jones looked like an older man but was younger than he looked. He was born somewhere on the east coast, maybe New Hampshire. No one knew for sure, not even he himself. The only thing he knew for sure was that his mother died of consumption and left him alone in the world when he was eleven. He was illiterate, penniless and had no trade. He migrated to the sea port of Mystic and started running with a gang of young ragtag misfits like himself. At fourteen he was hiding from the law and saw the sea as an escape route so he signed on as a whaler. He had his problems to be sure, he had little trust for any one, he was basically a loner but the sea life was for him. Many of his ship mates were loners too, they left each other space, like captured lions. He'd found a home and a lifestyle suited for him. He loved the adventure, not knowing or caring where he was heading, just as long as it was new.

This was his second voyage with the Captain and up until the shanghaiing mishap he was in good stead. He did not see that he was to fault. After all those scandals, those shanghais, had get him high on opium and them delivered those two while he was still opium stupid. They told him that they were both able body seamen. How was he to know that he was paying for a dying old man and a still wet behind the ears boy? It was not that Fredric was that young, hell he been that young when he'd gone to sea. It was that the boy was too educated and naive. He could see that the Captain was concerned regarding the boy's well-being. He'd given him a chose job, assisting the carpenter. That's cause the Captain felt that Fredric was too high class to be among the likes of him and Jones intended to bring Fredric down a notch or two. It seemed that Mr. Jones had this habit of blaming others for his misfortune.

As time went by, it became clear that Jones was intent upon provoking Fredric into a fight. To tell the truth, Fredric was a bit afraid of him.

Jones was not that tall but built stocky. He was probably 20 years Fredric's senior and 30 pounds heavier but still youthful enough to give one hell of a fight. Fredric was able avoid the confrontation for a time by keeping distance between them. In some way, this worked to his advantage by giving Jones the notion that Fredric would not fight. Fredric realized that sooner or later the fight was inevitable. He also understood that Jones was dangerous and he should not underestimate him. Fredric just wished Jones would just let it be. Fredric resolved to fight him only if he had to but then on his terms.

One afternoon while they were at a work party, cleaning the large copper kettles used for reducing whale blubber to oil, Jones became particle abusive and cocky and Fredric decided that he'd had enough. There were three men assigned to that duty, Jones, Fredric and Johnson, a neutral with regards to hostilities.

The First Mate had deck duty and Fredric was counting on him to intervene before the fight became deadly. Jones shoved him once too often and Fredric returned the shove. Jones wheeled to strike him with the 3 foot long, club like, wooden handle of the cleaning brush but Fredric instinctively side stepped the blow and struck back with his brush, the heavy wooden handle struck Jones in the face, just above his right eye, which knock him over and in to the kettles.

Jones rolled over, pushed the kettles aside and started to get to his feet, knife in hand. Fredric struck him in the rib cage with the brush breaking a rib. The pain was so severe that Jones doubled over and dropped the knife.

The adrenaline now surged through Fredric, the Thomas's stuff and endless harassing, boiled up and Fredric wanted to hurt him badly. Jones, his face covered with blood and in major pain, could see anger in Fredric's face. Fear began to rule and he started scrambling, crawling about looking for someplace to hide. At this point Fredric's youth and inexperience caused him to back off for a moment, the First Mate yelled to stop the fighting and restrained Fredric. This allowed Jones to recoup, get to his knees and sneak a blow to Fredric's back. Fredric pitched forward and fell into the kettles. Before Jones could strike again, the First Mate grabbed him in a choke hold and drove his head hard against the copper kettles. Then he told Jones that he made a big mistake. The Captain had told him to look after Fredric and this did not look good. He told Jones to back off and then released him.

Jones hesitated for a moment then grabbed a cleaning brush and struck out at Fredric but the first mate was able to seize his arm yielding the blow ineffective. He threw Jones to the deck, placing his heavy boot squarely on his chest. At this point the pain overwhelmed Jones's desire to fight; he uttered a few choice words, groaned as his hand relaxed, dropping the wooden handled brush.

Fredric had gained significant status and respect by establishing that he could and would fight you if you push him too far. Jones on the other hand had proved that he was untrustworthy, that given the chance would stab you in the back. Whaling was a business, about making money and they needed every able body man, even the Joneses. Once the First Mate told you to back off, that was the law and you better obey it or invoke the consequences. The First Mate then told Jones that he got what he'd asked for and by god that will be the end of it. But Jones was not about to forget the beating, the lost status and Fredric knew it and in fact he wished they could finish the fight right now, right here.

The Kill

The conflict between Jones and Fredric had been placed on the back burner with the crew preparing for the hunt. The crew grew restless with anticipation. Even Fredric was excited about his first hunt. They had seen other whalers in the area and felt sure that they would spot one soon. Then the lookout called out "there she blows". Then the Coxswain hollered, "Where". "Three of them, four points to the port. About a mile" the lookout yelled. "Keep your eye on them and sing out when we are true" calls out the Coxswain. The deck mate ordered the deckhands to ready the boats. The three whales, probably a pod of related animals, were swimming leisurely as the La Ninfa closed in. At about a half a mile distance, the Captain ordered the whaling boats lowered.

Fredric watched as the boats rowed off towards the whales. The Captain was manning the front boat, followed closely by Orrick commanding the second boat and then the First Mate in charge of the third boat. A good two thirds of the crew was on the boats. The pod was swimming leisurely, blowing now and again, diving with their tails in the air, and then surfacing for a while. The boats fan out with the Captain's boat in the center. The Coxswain was steering the ship under the directions of the lookout towards the whales. Seamen were trimming the sails.

Then Orrick struck the trailing whale with a true shot. The Captain harpooned soon followed then struck the whale high on its back. The Captain and Orrick nearly collided as the whale in terror began to swim wildly in an attempt to escape. The third boat laid off and waited to assist where necessary.

The whale fought valiantly but in vain. What seemed like an hour but was closer to two the whale began to tired and Orrick was able to lance it several times, blood began to exit from the blow hole as the last bit of life escaped and the kill was complete. The whale then rolled over and they were able to fasten a hawser around its flunks. What had been a beautiful living creature an hour or so ago was now on its back being towed towards La Ninfa. Orrick with the First Mated help chain the whale to the side of the ship. Without waiting for the Captain to return, the men prepared to strip the blubber from the catch. The cooper passed them the long handled spades used to cut the blubber into long strips. Men aboard cut the strips into chunks and throw them into the waiting kettles. Fredric was busy manning the kettles and loading the blubber and did not see the Captain return but then noticed that he was working alongside the crew.

Every man including the officers worked to process the whale. They worked nonstop into the evening but still could not complete the process. The wind had picked up and water was breaking over the wells. The

Captain ordered the crew aboard and to prepare the ship for foul weather. They had to ride out the weather for two days before they could return to the task.

They worked a day and half cutting, boiling and filling caskets with oil. They stored the baleen, kettles and caskets of oil. The Captain ordered a portion of rum for each man to celebrate the kill. The men all gathered about the Captain and saluted with their mugs, all except Jones. He was nowhere to be found. He'd disappeared sometime in the past three days. He was not the first sailor nor the last to mysteriously disappear at sea. But then he did not have any friends that mourned his demise.

Chapter 13
Midshipman

Isla 1865 - 1902

Isla had thought seriously of jumping overboard when the La Ninfa was in San Francisco Bay and swimming for shore. She was nearly fifteen with hormones pumping through her young body. She'd been aboard this ship since forever, well maybe more like three years but long enough to go through puberty, to change from girl to a woman with a body with all the female shapes. Her only company was her family and ship's officers, a bunch of old men. She was forbidden to talk to the crew or go for a walk about the ship without her mother. Her wardrobe was limited and out of style, it consisted only of what she could pack in a small sea chest. She fought constantly with her sister and refused to do her studies, especially the bible studies, which stressed her mother to no end.

When she saw and heard that beautiful young men speak in Latin, it was love at first sight and she was determined to see him again. She began demanding that he tutor her in Latin and if she could not get her way she'd commit suicide. The Nelson family life was in disarray and Martha, the Captain's wife, believed the only way to restore harmony was to compromise and allow Fredric to tutor her. But not alone, he has to tutor the two girls together and then only for an hour a day under her supervision. He would be forbidden to socialize with girls or see them except when tutoring.

Martha presented her husband with an option, go along with the plan or face possible loss of this family. She told him life was unbearable and this was one option, the other was to bring them ashore. Martha did not speak in this manner unless she meant it. The Captain was willing to allow Fredric to tutor the girls but there was an issue.

He could not allow a member of the crew to fraternize with his family, it would break protocol and could result in loss of discipline. The solution was to promote Fredric to midshipmen and have him quarter with the officers. Besides the boy seemed bright, well educated and the navigation officer could use an assistant.

Accidentel pourboire

Chapter 14
Gift of Life

Destiny

E ffie's period was late but she was a woman in her mid-thirties and assumed it had something to do with the change of life. And besides, she only had intercourse with one male recently and he was just a boy. As the weeks passed and still no period she thought of buying that Chinese herbal concoction that would induce miscarriages just in case. But again she ascribed it to her age, not to being pregnant. She was childless and never wanted to bear a child Yet there was something going on inside her body.

The beautiful fall San Francisco days were so beautiful and the French Food at Perrier was better than ever. While taking a carriage ride about Golden Gate Park, she found herself thinking about babies. That surprised her so much that she decided for sure to take some of that herbal stuff. But her outlook on life was changing. With her child bearing years slipping away, her youth was fading, how quickly the years had passed and now with old age stalking her, she no longer looked at life as never ending but now as a limited quantity to be valued and used wisely. For the first time in her life the thought of a new life sent tingles through her. At that moment she knew that if possible, she'd have this child.

92

She named him Montgomery Gregory in honor of Sarah and herself. She always called him Monty. She spent most of her time caring for Monty and left the day to day operation of the Bells Union to Jefferson, her long time manager. She took great pleasure in breast feeding him even though it was out of fashion. The next few years were the best of her life. She lived for her son, spoke to him in French and taught him to ride horses in the European fashion. But she had a major dilemma, she was well known as the madam of the Bells Union and she did not want her son to be known as the Madam's son. She considered moving to Europe and raising him there but could not bear the thought of returning to that socially stratified environment. They would always be considered up shots at best and more likely trashy commoners. Here in America he had the chance to be whatever he wanted. So with the help of some influential contacts, she got him accepted in Howe, a fine eastern Boarding School. It was the hardest thing she has ever done, even harder than burying Sarah. From the day she kissed him goodbye and turned him over to the headmistress at Howe until the day she died, she wept inside.

Fulfillment

A lifetime is not a fixed quantity and should only be measured in fulfillment. When a child dies the sense of loss is great, it dies in the spring of life without a chance to fulfill life's promise. When an older person dies the loss is less, they had their four seasons. And if they were not prudent and died unfulfilled, then that is their loss. It is natural to do a self-appraisal periodically but as you grow older it is almost a daily event, that is because you are acutely aware of the passage of time. It seemed that when you were young you could afford to spend a few years here and there but when you're on the home stretch, you just do not have any time to spare.

Effie's health was failing and it was time to bring her son home. Her business affairs had gone badly the past years and she had to sell the Bella Union. She could not afford to keep Monty in school any longer. She hoped she'd live long enough to see him again. She knew he'd be so handsome. But just in case she'd written a letter that talked about his father and his grandmother. It was to be given to him when he arrived. She also sent a letter to Chris Davison whom she understood was Monty's real grandfather. There would not be significant funds in her estate so he needed to secure a job. She hoped that his grandfather would give him work at the Tavern and look after him until he was able to care for himself. In any case, his well being would soon be out of her hands; the Doctors gave her only a few days. With her weakened heart her body could not fight off the pneumonia that was consuming her lungs. As she thought about her life she had many regrets but Monty was not one of them. As life ebbed away, Sarah came to meet her. She held her hand and told her that her mother was waiting to see her.

Day 12 Military Medals

*A*nother day, another dollar, as they say. I spent another night in the quarters above the saloon. It was becoming more like home. Someone was knocking on the doors again. Can't they read CLOSED UNTIL FURTHER NOTICE. Standing at the doorstep was a elderly woman. As I opened the door she took a step backward, examined me and asked "When are you going to open"? It seems to me that I'd seen this same woman from my youth, wearing the same clothes.

This lady was dressed in an ankle length floral paisley dress, black sturdy looking shoe, and a flat looking hat that partially covered her gray neatly combed hair. She was hanging onto the straps of a small black handbag.

But how could that be I asked myself? She looked to be in her late sixties and the woman I remember from my youth would be much older, say 100 years. Then it came to me. This woman had simply replaced the woman I remember from my youth. It occurred to me that people move through life in discrete steps and change the uniform accordingly. That thirty years ago she would have worn the uniform of a younger woman and another woman, probably long gone, had worn the old woman's uniform. Each generation just pops from one stage to another. It's kind of like flipping through a book of life and the characters move from page to page wearing the appropriate uniforms.

"I know you, " she said, still examining me with a scolding expression. "You're little Johnny, I heard you had gone into the military. Are you the one that fought in the Philippines"?

"No mam, that I believe was my grandfather, and that was long before my time. But the answer to your question is I do not intend to open soon or ever". I said.

"Well this generation has no ambition, not like mine. Heck, we'd walk a mile in the snow to earn a penny". She said as she turned and walked away in a huff.

Day 13 Closer look

*T*he day after her visit I decided to take a closer look at the contents of Sarah's Hand Bag. I had remembered that there were a couple of old Military Medals and wanted to really look at them. One was read, "Philippine Campaign 1899-1903 and the other "Philippine Insurrection 1899."

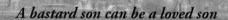
Chapter 15
Destiny is a Joker

A Child of Privilege Montgomery Gregory 1880-1937

Montgomery, Monty for short, was one of those privileged children that lived at Howe, a fine Eastern Military Boarding School. His father, whom he never knew, had been lost at sea while returning to San Francisco from a business trip. He thought that he'd been in the Railroad business or something, he really did not know for sure. Be that as it may, he apparently had made a lot of money, money enough to allow his widow to live well and send him to a fine school. Before he went away to school he lived with his mother in a fine hotel somewhere in San Francisco. Where he was not sure because he was so young then and could only remember how beautiful it was.

At first, he'd missed his mother very much but as time went by, he grew accustomed to life at Howe. She and San Francisco became a distant memory, almost like one of those dreams that are hard to discern from actual life. He accelerated in both academics and sports and was highly thought of by his classmates. He envisioned attending an Ivy League College and then possibly practicing law or politics but not a military career. He wanted to live somewhere in the East, god knows he did not want to live on the West Coast. It was still quite crude there. He was in his senior year at Howe when he received the latter summoning him home.

Presidio Real de San Francisco

For the last hundred million years or so the tectonic motion of the earth's plates had deposited continental crust, known as the Franciscan Complex, on the edge of the North American Plate, much like plaster on the edge of a building. Much of the terrain, land or crust or if you like plaster on the side of the American plate was generated in subduction zones miles below the surface and then up-lifted to the surface. The terrain consists of many types of rocks, including chert, granite, and serpentine.

The granite and serpentine are magma that cooled before it reached the surface. The chert, layered rock, and serpentine which forms the underpinning of the peninsula is covered by sand, sand created by erosion of primeval mountains, carried by the ancient rivers, Sacramento and San Juan, down to the sea shore and then deposited by westerly winds back on to the land.

For the last few thousand years the Ohlone people occupied this peninsula and they had no knowledge of that nonsense, North American Plate. But what they believed was the bay was created by a deity for their people. Before the bay a pleasant valley existed, protected from the ocean weather by a mountain ridge. Perhaps or not but one story has it that this deity accidentally or intentionally punched a break in the ridge, created the bay. One thing for sure they did not need Father Sierra protection. They were doing just fine and lived in small groups along the peninsula, fished, hunted and gathered for a livelihood.

Their lives changed, in particularly the group living along the marshlands near the entrance to the bay. In 1776 when Juan Bautista de Anza selected their ancestral ground for the site of a military fort and Jose Joaquin Moraga set up camp, El Presidio Real de San Francisco, on the wind sweep slopes above the serpentine cliffs near the present day Golden Gate Bridge. They lost their land and their freedom because the Spanish government in Mexico City, fearing the encroachment of Yankees, decided to establish a military and civilian settlement on the peninsula.

The Ohlone people, their souls and much of their land was placed under the church authority for safe keeping, to be returned when their culture matured, adulthood so to speak.

With the Mexican independence and Secularization, their land was confiscated, mostly for land grants, and they and their souls were cast a drift rarely to be thought of again. Twenty four years after the Mexican revolution, the Presidio changed hands again when the Yankees took control. In the late nineteenth hundreds when war broke out with Spain, the Presidio was only a frontier military outpost, ill equipped to handle the influx of soldiers headed for the Philippines. The war changed it into a functioning military base.

In northeast Greece there was a city, Philippi, between the Adriatic coast and Byzantium. Like many ancient cities its name had changed. It was Krenides under the Thracians in the sixth century BC. Renamed in the fourth century B.C. by Philip H of Macedon for himself. He was the father of Alexander the Great and lucky that Alexander did not rename it Alexandra but perhaps that is because Alexander needed to make amends for Philip's untimely demise. In the first century B.C. Brutus and Cassius, the slayers of Julius Caesar, came out on the short end of a battle there and were decisively defeated by Antony and Octavian. Perhaps they thought of changing its name to Antonia or Octavian but this did not. It was still called Philippi and the site of Paul the apostle's favorite Christian church. But the Philippi in Macedon was not on the minds of the Yankees; it was the Philippine islands in the South Pacific, currently a Spanish possession that they coveted.

Homecoming

Monty sat dejected on the front steps of the Tavern. It had not opened but he had nowhere else to go. His mother had been buried yesterday and he was alone and penny-less in this world. As he sat there thinking about what a difference a few days made, just the other day he'd been the son of a Railroad tycoon and today he's the bastard son of a Tavern owner. A smartly dressed soldier broke his line of thought and handed him a flyer, "Remember the Main" was boldly printed in large letters across the top. The soldier told him that the army was looking for volunteers; the pay was good, he'd have food and shelter. Monty took the flyer, signed it and joined a few other young men in a back of a wagon. The wagon was a converted prairie schooner with facing benches. It was pulled by two strong Tennessee mules and driven by a black soldier, a buffalo soldier, the famed Indian fighters of the west, in a fine blue Cavalry uniform.

After a couple of hours, the addition of two more volunteer and lengthy trips about town the wagon headed due west over the old Spanish military road that connected the military camp with Fort Point. By the time the wagon reaches the Presidio, Monty's rear was sore, his legs were stiff and he'd had a change of mind But there was no going back, he was told in unambiguous terms that he was in the military and they owned his ass and soul until he was told something different.

Monty was assigned to Camp Merriam, named for the commanding general of the Department of California. The camp was near the eastern border of the Presidio, close to the Lombard Gate entrance. It housed the 1st. California Infantry and California Volunteers. The volunteers were issued uniforms, knapsack, three pairs of socks, two pairs of boots and a Model 1889 "trapdoor" Springfield and Krag rifle. This trapdoor model, single cartage load, had the new rod bayonet but was outdated in comparison with the smokeless powder weapons that were becoming available. Its main advantage was availability since the army had a stockpile of them.

The Volunteers were given basic training consisting mostly of marching drills, firing drills, bayonet drills and lots of mental abuse. The marching drills enable large numbers of men to move in an orderly efficient manner. The firing drills taught them to have a true aim.

Bayonet drill was just in case but they were told in today's combat with all its fire power, the bayonet is obsolete. Perhaps that is so but the instructor, a Buffalo Soldier, a veteran of the Indian Wars was quite familiar with the Model 1889 rifle, said "the bayonet just might well be the only thing between you and kingdom come. This is your weapon, learn to use it all, bayonet and butt". He proceeds to demonstrate alternate short jabs with the bayonet and control swings of the butt. "Do not get over committed, keep your balance and your senses about you". He always insisted on an extra 15 minutes of bayonet practice. The mental abuse that was handed out in ample quantities was designed to break down their civilian sensibility and create an obedience killer, because, after all that is what soldiers do, they kill when ordered.

The Zealandia

There have been many ships over the years named Zealandia, including a rather famous 6,683 ton multi-decked single-funnelled Australian cargo and passenger ship commissioned in 1910. This ship transported troops in the two great wars. The allies requisitioned her in 1918 to transport the American Expeditionary force to France. She was requisitioned again for WW2 and transports most of the ill fated Australian 8th division in the South Pacific Theater where most became Japanese prisoners of war and many died as prisoners of war. The Zealandia of the Spanish American War was another ship though, it was an Ironclad three mast clipper ship.

She was launched in 1869 in Glasgow at the C.Connell & CO yard. Like many ships of her period she had a copper lined hull. She had an official British Reg.No 60969 and was intended for the New Zealand trade. But since she was designed as a passenger ship, she ended up ferrying passengers, across both the Atlantic and Pacific oceans. By the time she was requisitioned for duty in the Spanish American War, she was a veteran of many sea voyages, obsolete but still a fine ship. In many respects she was a luxury liner compared to the typical troop transport.

It was unusually hot that May,1898 and when word came down that they would be shipping out the next day, the California Volunteers cheered loudly. They were tired of the camp routine and wanted to get down to the fighting business. They were fed breakfast at 4 A.M., broke camp by 6 A.M. and with knapsack and equipment marched the 5 miles to pier 7. The citizens of San Francisco came out in large numbers to cheer their boys on to war, so large in fact that it was difficult to find a marching room through the crowd. A company of the California Volunteers, Monty included and a company of the Pennsylvania Volunteers was assigned to the Zealandia. Aboard there was hot coffee and sandwiches for the boys served by the ladies of the Red Cross. There were farewell speeches, cheer and so on and then the civilians were ordered ashore, soldiers assigned bunks, the gang plank pulled and the Zealandia and a couple hundred soldiers set sail for the Philippines.

Philippine A Pacific Cruise 1889

The talk aboard was that this was going to be a cake walk. The boys had heard about the rout in Cuba and of the defeat of the Spanish fleet by Commodore George Dewey. Heck, all they got to do is take a Pacific cruise, round up a few rebels and be home by Christmas. The Zealandia arrived in the Philippines on June 30th; Monty along with the rest of the company joined the main body of 1st California volunteers. Because of Monty's military schooling and natural leadership skills, he was given a field commission, second lieutenant, and put in command of a rifle platoon, the point of the spear.

The California volunteers took up a position outside Manila which was under rebel control. In the push into the city in August, Monty's platoon took a point position and encountered heavy resistance. At one point in the fighting, his platoon was nearly run over. He gave the order to take up defensive positions, to mount bayonets and hold their ground no matter what, any retreat at that time would have resulted in heavy casualties and possibly complete annihilation. Their rifles with the trapdoor loading could not be reloaded and fired quickly enough to fend off the enemy and they were forced into hand-to-hand type combat. They were fortunate that the Filipinos too were poorly equipped and did not have the superior Mauser magazine rifles as did the Spanish. In fact, the rebel that engaged Monty's troops had few firearms and fought mostly with swords, knives and machetes.

This was not the combat that the Volunteers expected nor were trained for, not the distant killing of nineteen century engagement but the close-up man to man fighting of warriors with clashing bodies, sweat, blood, screams, anger, pain, and fear which together sounded like a primeval howl. Men fought on even when severely injured, used dead comrades as shields, rifles as clubs, butt and bayonet like gladiators; it was a matter of life or death. Not just their life but the lives of their buddies right next to them. They were no longer fighting to avenge the Main but for self-preservation. The platoon fought as a team with Monty constantly rallying, galvanizing them to prevent panic and hold their ground. To panic, to lose control at that moment would have been a disaster for his platoon.

Much like a flock of sheep being attacked by a pack of wolves, they would have been slaughtered. Relief came when the rebels flank was breached by California Regulars forcing the rebels to retreat and regroup.

After the Battle

Of his twenty-man platoon, six were dead, another three died of their wounds and the rest, except one or two, the inevitable lucky few, were wounded to some extent. His regiment took part in the capture of Manila on August 13, 1898 but Monty and this platoon were not there, they were held back as reserves. Monty received a wound to his lower right leg. Most likely from glancing blows of machete or something. It was cleaned and treated at the base camp medical facilities. It seemed to be just a minor wound that would heal in due time but a persistent infection set in and he was finally hospitalized. In addition to that injury he had another wound of sorts, elucidation, a new scary perspective of himself and of life. It was not so visible but Monty would never again be that naiveté boy not after that type of combat.

For a short time during that man on man combat, he was free of inhabitation, allowed to unleash the primitive being, those instincts and adrenaline rush that must be subdued in a civilization. Words cannot fully describe this state of mind and are experienced by a few men. He would remember those brief moments that seem like an eternity as a highlight of his life.

For the rest of his life whenever he reflects on that event, he'd recoil at the memories of brutal killing but also feel the rush of freedom.

War Hero

Monty started out to avenge the Main, ending up being the vanguard of the projection of American power. The Filipinos, who had been fighting for their independence from the old weak declining Spanish Empire, now had to fight a new young rising

American Empire. The Filipinos put up a hell of a fight. It took three years of gorilla warfare and the capture of their leader, Emilio Aquinaldo to subdue them. First California Volunteer Infantry did not stay to witness that event but left the Philippines for the United States, arriving in the U.S. on August 24, 1899.

Monty did not return with his regiment but remained hospitalized. For over a year the doctor treated his wound without success and eventfully sent him to the Presidio for further testament. He did not return to San Francisco and the cheering crowds as did his regiment but only to a staff nurse and a waiting ambulance.

He was a veteran and had a regular army Captain's commission but he also had a badly wounded leg that would not heal. The medical staff at the Presidio found him not fit for service and summarily discharged him. So at twenty one with a bad leg and two service medals, he was once again back in San Francisco with nowhere to go.

Chapter 16
The family

The Family Redemption 1899

A t first Chris did not pay much attention to the young man sitting on the steps of the Tavern, it was not unusual to see a down and out, even in Army Uniform loitering about the bar looking for a handout. But there seemed to be something familiar about him. The way he held his head reminded Chris of his father. For some unknown reason, Chris began thinking about the letter and subsequent conversations with Effie Gregory about her son fathered by Fredric. He anticipated seeing the boy after Effie's funeral a few years ago but nothing came of it. He'd heard that the boy had enlisted but that's about all.

Chris was getting along in years and like most men began to worry about his legacy. He felt more and more guilt with regards to Fredric. He'd abandon him at birth and could not rescue him from the shanghaiers. Perhaps to make amends for this and many other deeds, he decided to assist this young soldier. But perhaps there was more.

Could he be the boy? Chris, without knowing why said "Montgomery"! He'd remembered the name because Montgomery was Sarah's last name. Montgomery Gregory was the name of the boy that was reported to be his grandson through Fredric. In a way Chris had always known this day would come, that sooner or later he'd meet him. The young man raised his head and looked at him for a moment and said "Grandfather, I could use some help". It seemed so strange that two men that had never met instantly recognized each other as blood relatives. Chris did not have to ask why because he could see by the glassed over eyes that he was quite ill. Chris took him to Fredric's old room upstairs above the bar. It had been empty for years, ever since the night Fredric was shanghaied.

As soon as Chris saw Monty's leg he knew he must act quickly to save his life. Chris has seen similar infections as a boy in West Virginia and knew how to treat them. The first order of business was to open the wound and with hot packs drain and draw the blood poison back down the leg. Then, go after the source of the infection. The old Indian squaw back home would make a compact of a yellowish greenish earth, mashed Indian Soap (an onion like plant readily available in the area) and water. She'd place the mixture over the wound and allow it to dry. She said that the mud composition drew the poison out of the wound while it dried. She'd repeat the process unit the red line extending from the wound was gone. Chris understood that the yellowish greenish stuff was sulfur rich soil, and he'd seen similar material in Chinese herbal shops. Chris paid a local boy to dig up a few Indian Soap bulbs and fetch some sulfur rich earth from a Chinese herb store. Maria, Giovanni's oldest daughter volunteered to act as his nurse and mix up and replace the compacts as soon one would dry.

The combination of Chris's medicine and Maria's loving touch cured in a few weeks what the army doctor could not in months. Not only was Monty becoming healthy but he also was falling in love. Maria was also falling in love with Monty but could not express it because she was a married woman. She was only nineteen but had married at seventeen, not really that young in those days. She'd married a man against her father's advice. He said he was nothing but Pacheco, a bad man. She knew that if she returned Monty's love, that there would be deadly consequences.

Not Be Denied

But their love would not be denied and they began having an affair which soon became apparent to all including Maria's husband, Elgin. Elgin, a product of a hard living Polish immigrant and a first generation Russian Jewish mother, was not the type of man to cross, especially if it involved love and ego. While Elgin was baptized a Catholic, why his father bothered was a mystery since he neither practices the religion or for that matter believed in god, and raised faithless. Ruth, his mother, a large boned strong peasant type, was more than practicing Jew, she was a passionate believer.

Perhaps Elgin's father baptized him to prevent his mother from raising him to be a good Jew. The plan seemed to work because Elgin was a tough and ruthless man. He started as an apprentice to his father's trade, strong arm protection racket, while still in grade school. By the time he was twenty he'd established his own protection racket and a reputation as a businessman, a ladies man and a man to be feared. He was terribly handsome with a rugged bold face, unforgiving blue eyes, bushy blond hair, a strong muscular body, thanks to his mother genes, and little or no ramose, thanks to his father.

The type of a bad man a young rebellious woman might fall in love with. The kind of man she might see as the opposite of her docile family-man father. Elgin was an exciting man who commanded respect wherever he went and could and would lavish her with gifts. No longer would she have to do menials house chores and be expected to have a score of kids.

Chris, her father's boss was one of Elgin's clients and she'd seen him many times over the years while helping her father clean up the bar. He usually came in the morning just after it opened. He was always dressed so well, classy, and often had a beautiful young lady with him. He always bought everyone in the bar a drink. He winked at her and gave her a silver dollar.

She could tell that Chris and her father did not like him but nonetheless Chris always had an envelope ready for him. He'd take the envelope order another round of drinks and leave without paying for the drinks or saying thanks for the envelope. He was much older and while she admired him from afar she never thought of him in romantic terms but rather just as an older man. But as she began to develop in her teens she noticed a change in the way that he addressed her. He was quite charming in a playful manner. He always treated her in a respectful way, almost as an adult, not as a child like her parents. Her attitude toward him began to change and she thought she was in love with him. They had a few secret meetings and she was overwhelmed by him, after all he was a worldly man who commanded respect with a great deal of experience and knowledge regarding women and she loved it.

Father's Love

They were married in the old Saint Mary cathedral and celebrated the Liturgy together. He treated her as a goddess, almost untouchable and that's where things started going badly. She was a healthy young woman with strong sexual desires, a need for affection and companionship not a doll to be placed on a pedestal. Her desire for a real husband and her hard head propelled her into inevitable conflict that resulted in physical fights. Elgin could not and would not be bothered. After all, a woman should obey her husband and appreciate the things he gave her.

From his standpoint, the only way to treat an ungrateful woman was to beat her into submission. This approach only worsened the situation and so Maria moved back home to her father's house after only three months of marriage. This move put Elgin and her father on a collision course, Giovanni could not and would not expose his daughter to that type of treatment. And then the affair with Monty started and Giovanni knew that a deadly confrontation was inevitable.

Elgin emerged from the basement opium den, still in an opium stupor. It was his custom to indulge in the physical pleasures, women and drugs on a regular basis. He particularly liked and patronized the establishments on Wentworth Alley. For Elgin too regularly, since he could easily be found if one chose to. Elgin paid little attention to the calls, rags, bottles, sacks, rags bottles sacks, of the junkman. Nor was he concerned when the wagon stopped as he walked down the Alley. With the precision of a professional killer, Giovanni slipped the cord over this head and tightened it about his neck with unforgiving strength. The force was so strong that the cord cut deep into Elgin's throat. This force was generated from the hate of a father and the distaste of a working man for a parasite. What seemed like a very long time after Elgin went limp, perhaps to be sure that he was dead or perhaps because it took that long for the hate to subside, Giovanni maintained the stranglehold. Then he heaved the body like so much junk into the wagon and covered it with rags, sacks and bottles. The body was loaded onto a fishing boat and then dumps somewhere north of the Gate. No one seemed to notice or care when Elgin came up missing. There might have been some observers outside the opium- den but this was Wentworth Alley in China Town and the Chinese had learned not to see when necessary, especially when it concerned white people. And as for the boat crew, blood is thicker than water and never more true than with the Italians.

Family Man: Lloyd Francis Montgomery 1903-1921, Paul Giovanni Montgomery 1905-1967, Albertina Maria Montgomery 1908-1988

There is nothing much better than an Italian wedding except perhaps an Italian christening. Maria did not want to marry again in the church but it was important to her father and after all if it had not been for his love, she might have been attending Monty's funeral. And of course, when Giovanni's first grandchild, a healthy boy weighing 9 pounds 10 ounce, named Lloyd after Robert Lloyd the English poet, was born three months early, the first child quite often arrives early, Giovanni invites most of North Beach to celebrate at Tavern. Paul, for St Paul the apostle, a full-term baby followed in 1905. Then in 1908 came Albertina, just because Maria likes the name, again a full-term baby. And so by 1908 the child of privilege, the bastard, the warrior was a husband, a father and a full time bar keeper. He was a family man first and made sure to celebrate all the life events, birthdays, first communion, graduations, anniversaries and so on and always in the Tavern. He'd close it down, invite the whole family and more and always have plenty of cold meats, bread, pasta and spirits. Next to those few minutes of life-threatening combat in the Philippines, these were the highlight of his life.

1906 Changing of the guard

April 20th, the fire had been raging on for almost two days. Despite the mayor Schmitz's wish-full thinking and General Funston's best effort the city seemed doomed. But when the smoke cleared, they were able to save half the city and most of the saloons, the Tavern included. To minimize looting and ensure the safety of the citizens, the Mayor and the General closed all the saloons and authorized the militia to patrol the streets. They were able to shoot about 500 people and keep the bars closed for sixty days. The militia was soon retired and despite the best efforts of the Temperance lobbied the saloons, including the Tavern reopened on July 5, 1906. When it reopened the Tavern had a new owner, Monty, Chris's grandson. It would have made a great story if Chris had died in the great San Francisco earthquake and fire but this was not the case.

Day 14 The old yellowed Newspaper

I was sitting in my usual spot behind the bar in an evening day dream and thinking about Georgia in that summer dress. I began to scold myself. You dummy, your path to freedom awaits you. You can break loose from this hum dum life, escape to paradise just as you have always wanted. No but not you dummy! you're letting a lady young enough to be your daughter into your mind. Perhaps you need to be reminded of the pain it can bring. You're foot free and fancy, just use your head, sell the place, take the money and proceed to paradise. Now if only I knew where paradise is.

With nothing better to do I started to think about the old newspaper in the safe. Why would anyone save a newspaper with a story about some murder?

Chapter 17
Chris's Return 1906

The doctor attributed his somewhat early demise to heart congestion but the most likely cause was boredom. Well not simple boredom but boredom resulting from the loss of physical prowess. They say the legs are the first to go and that may be so but sight, hearing and sexual capabilities are not far behind. So Chris did what most old men want to do, put his house in order before the sins of his youth caught up with him. He felt that it was important to locate Fredric and if not then leave a written record for Fredric whom he was sure would show up some time. He wrote the details of his life in a journal. When he was satisfied with his documentary chore, he decided that he must say goodbye to David. He left the Tavern to Monty with the understanding that when Fredric showed up they would be partners. He left the journal and Sarah's handbag with Monty for safekeeping. He knew one day Fredric would return to San Francisco and he had so much to tell him.

Virginia City

He made the return journey to Virginia City. The glory days were gone and the City streets were no longer jammed with miners, gamblers and hustlers. Gone was the endless line of teamsters with their wagons filled with mining supplies and such. It was early, only 10 AM but still in the old days wagons would be lined up clear past Gold Hill by this time. The Opera House had been closed for a number of years and only a few stores and bars remained open. The Delta Saloon, in disrepair with cracked windows and faded paint, a shadow of its former self, was still in operation. He'd heard that it survived the great fire of 75. Chris (Jack) peered through the swinging doors and could see a few men at the bar. He thought he recognized one of them, a former associate in the stock business. Chris hesitated then pushed open the doors, the familiar smell of alcohol and stale tobacco evoked a flood of memories, worm memories of his youth, of the glory days of David, of Catherine and nightmarish memories of that night and Addison.

After a moment of reflections, Chris took a closer look at the man. He was shorter, fatter and of course older than Chris remembered but it was him, Dead Eye Charles. They called him Dead Eye not because he was crack shot but because he had a lazy eye. His reddish complexion and glossed over eyes were the testament to his quest for happiness or at least relief through the bottle. At first the man did not recognize Chris but then, almost dropping his drink, he said "I heard you were dead". Chris smiled, "I thought I was; how are you Charles?" then order two drinks, neat shots of whiskey. They touched glass, took long moments, eye to eye appraisal and downed their shots. Charles began to talk about the old days. He told Chris that Catherine had never married, had retired years ago and moved east. He said that David and Addison were buried in the same cemetery, only yards apart; that it was easy to find Addison's because he had the largest marker, a marble weeping angel, in the place. Catherine had had it made especially for him. Their graves were not in the main cemetery but in the smaller one near Ophir Ravine just above the City.

Only Gods Can Forgive

It was late autumn and a burst of chilly wind drove red dust and yellow cottonwood leaves down the dirt road leading to the cemetery.

There were so many graves in disorder there, forlorn and forgotten. Most of the graves were without markers or only with weathered and unreadable wooden markers. Just as Dead Eye Charles had said, Addison grave was easy to spot. The Weeping Angel, tilted to one side due to the decaying of the coffin and such, her fine features no longer shiny but dulled with age and she had dark moss spots growing on her. The inscription read "Addison Jefferson Whitfield A Son of the South who survived many a battle just to be struck down in the prime of life by an assassin's blade."

After a great deal of work and some good fortune he was able to locate David's grave. It was marked by a weathered wooden headboard. It was just legible. The lightly painted white letters were embossed above the weathered eroded wooden plank and read "DAVID You Will Be Missed" " MAY GOD FORGIVE YOU". As Chris read, he thought "David can you forgive me? For I cannot forgive myself. You were like a father to me and I was your executioner". Chris hoped that his visit would relieve him of the pain, the guilt he's endured all these years; but to no avail, for he would have to live with the consequence of that stupid deed till the day he dies.

Fortunately for Chris, now going by Jack, that was not that long. To Jack the best years of his life were here in Virginia City and he decided the last days of his life were going to be here. He made the arrangements to be buried next to David and as many a man before him have, kind of willed himself to die. Only Charles and three grave diggers were there to witness the burial. Dead Eye Charles made a toast to Jack, David and the glory days of yesteryear and emptied, after passing the bottle and taking a large swig himself, a bottle of fine Bourbon on their graves.

Day 15 Grandfather like Grandson

I started thinking about my Grandfather's Hong Kong journal and my liberty time there. For American sailors only Cinderella Liberty, had to be back on board the ship by midnight, was granted. Hong Kong has been under British control for years, had a large English speaking community, a large American presence and a British military base. If you stayed in the British areas it was quite safe and pleasant. There were a number of bars that were frequented by American sailors, one in particular was the White Horse. The US dollar was strong and went a long way. We did not actually have dollars, we had a military script and it was readily accepted.

I thought maybe after I sold the Tavern I might move to Hong Kong, like Grandfather Fredric had, and lived there for a while.

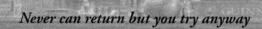
Chapter 18
Prodigal Son Returns 1907

The John Company

The British East Indian Company, John Company as it was commonly called, was a joint stock company established in the 1600s. It had a Royal Charter granted by Elizabeth I and had prospered for over two centuries before it was dissolved. It probably would still be in business if it had remained just a trading company but in an effort to maximize profit, the John Company became an auxiliary government that ruled India for a profit and for some pleasure. Finally in the mid nineteenth century the Indian peasant had enough of the Company's maximizing profit and rebelled. The rebellion, Sepoy Mutiny, of 1857 resulted in its demise.

While the company was dissolved in 58, many of its assets such as ships were owned by individuals and they continued to sail the old trade routes.

Fives and Tens

Some say at forty, your perspective of life changes but it can occur any time that you can see both sides of the picture. You will note that life goes by in fives and tens, ten years before you are dry between the ears, five through puberty, another five years getting your feet on the ground and so on. So one day life appears to be slipping away and you say. What now? And so was the case with Fredric Jack Wagner. He thought about how fast the years have passed, about all the ports he'd seen and the people he'd met over the years.

He thought about Isla, the many happy years and the fine little family they had. Even now it was difficult to accept and impossible to understand how quickly life can change. They had a fine house in the English section of Hong Kong. Her father, Mr. Nelson, had joined up with his brother-in-law in a trading business in Hong Kong and had settled there with his family. He, Mr. Nelson had to give up the whaling business, pretty much under a direct order from his wife or face the consequences. He sold La Ninfa and invested the proceeds in his brother-in-law's trading company that became quite successful. Fredric had worked for Mr. Nelson for a few years and earned a handsome wage.

He'd married Isla after a short engagement and they bought a fine house close to Mr. Nelson's home. But the sea was in his blood now. Fredric had tasted the adventure of the sea and soon returned to it, leaving his wife for extended periods. Isla had accepted his decision but anticipated that it was only temporary and that he'd eventually return to his job there in Hong Kong.

The 1475-ton square rigged merchant ship, 'Warley', an old John Company ship, which Mr. Nelson owned a share of, was now under the command of Fredric, his son in-law. The Warley was built at John Perry's yard at Blackwall in 1795. The ship routinely sailed between England and Hong Kong. The Warley was en route to England when Fredric received the message regarding his family. The message did not arrive until a month after the fact. Isla and his daughter had succumbed to the 1902 typhoid epidemic that swept through Hong Kong. He still feels guilty and is sure that he had done something to evoke the raft of the gods. He returned to Hong Kong only once to say a prayer,   not really a prayer but more like a goodbye, at their grave sites and bid farewell to the Nelson family. His home became the sea and for the next few years, he only left the ship long enough to get drunk. But the days of the sailing ships were going and Warley was deemed obsolete and sold to an Indian merchant in Bomb Bay. He did not like the new steams ship and so after delivering the

Warley, he chose to leave the sea. He booked passage on a German iron hull clipper from Bomb Bay to San Francisco.

Can Never Return

It had been a long time since Fredric had been in San Francisco. He'd spend so many years as a sailor. First with the whaling fleet and then in the British commercial fleet. The city had gone through some dramatic change, not only because of the earthquake but also the business climate. It seemed that there was construction going on everywhere. Not only the reconstruction of the earthquake and fire damage but also new stuff. Many of the street names had changed; DuPont was now Grant and the Montgomery extensions was now Columbus. There were a surprising number of automobiles on the streets. The horses and horse drawn wagons were still in evidence but it was clear the autos were the wave of the future. The whalers and the shanghais were pretty much gone now but the gamblers and the hookers were still going strong. As he headed up Kerry past Portsmouth Square, his thoughts drifted back to those events, realization about his biological parents and being shanghaied many years ago. His thoughts switch to his biological father and how he'd hated him. He wondered about his mother, what had become of her? He thought about Effie, what strange encounter that was. He had always wondered why he was never allowed to see her after that night. He wondered if the Bella Union was still in business and thought about going there but first he'd attend to his business at the Tavern.

Father and Son

He ordered whisky straight up, stood at the bar with one leg on the rail and looked around the bar. It seemed as if time had stood still here inside the Tavern. As he looked about, his attention returned to the bartender, yes it was Giovanni, his boyhood friend, he was sure of it. He said "hello Giovanni, how are you"?

Recognition slowly replaced surprise, Giovanni walked around the bar, looked Fredric over for a long moment, wrapped his arms around him and said, "I'd heard that you were still alive, god it's good to see you". The young man behind the bar looked on with some curiosity at this encounter as he continued cleaning up. After a moment or so Giovanni glanced toward the young man and then turned pointing towards him said "Fredric let me introduce my boss, my brother in-law and your son, Montgomery Gregory".

Chapter 19
An Outsider

The Exposition

While Europe engaged in a murderous continental struggle which started with the assassination of the heir to the Austrian Empire, Franz Ferdinand, in Sarajevo, the capital of Bosnia, San Francisco put the finishing touches on the grand fair. The Panama Pacific International Exposition was one grand exciting sight back in 1915. The city fought hard to be selected for the Exposition. Its main rival was New Orleans but San Francisco lobbied, spent big bucks and was proclaimed the host city by President Taft himself. Pacific International Exposition was officially a celebration of the opening of the Panama Canal. Pacific International Exposition took close to three years and a lot of money, about seventeen million, to build the six hundred odd acres fairs. It was a statement that San Francisco was back, that the Earth Quake and Fire was in the past.

For the better part of 1915, San Francisco's Panama Pacific International Exposition was open for business and saw 18 million odd visitors, close to 100 times the city population. The most popular site, the Tower of Jewels, stood better than 400 feet tall and was decorated with 10 thousands small colored gems, nova gems which were made in Bohemia. The last shipment of 5 thousand gems just escaped the war embargo imposed by Austria. At night these gems were illuminated by powerful searchlights. Another popular site was the Palace of Fine Art which exhibited the work of contemporary artists. Just to the west of the Palace and across the street, "The Avenue of Nations" was the Japanese exhibit. While it was not one of the major exhibits, it was probably the most serene. The Japanese constructed an exquisite garden, temples and tea pavilions.

They incorporated bamboo, dwarfed trees and a running brook. A portion of that exhibit still exists, not in the city but thirty or so odd miles down the peninsula. It sits on the eastern slope of the hills that separate the old Alameda de Las Pulgas, the main road of the Rancho de Las Pulgas, from the bay. The Rancho was a land grant of 35 thousand acres awarded to presidio comandante Don Jose Dario Arguello in 1795. Many years later, after the Exposition was closed, the tea pavilion were transported by barge down the bay and hauled up the hill side. It operated as a speakeasy, a brothel and now as a restaurant.

The Grandfather

Fredric took great pleasure in visiting the fair and it gave him a respite from his boring existence. Oh of course he had his new family here in San Francisco but then again it was his son, Monty's family and he was delegated to a grandfather's roll. He was much too young and strong, if not in age but in mind, to live that sedate life. The Japanese exhibit was Fredric's favorite. It was almost magical to step out of the hustle bustle of the Exposition into the tranquil peace of the garden and Fredric returned time and time again. It had been a number of years since he'd returned to San Francisco but he still felt a stranger. While he had no doubt that Monty was his son, he did not, could not feel close to him. He'd go to family dinners at Monty's home above the Tavern and the kids call him grandpa and yet he felt like an outsider. Well there was Lloyd, the oldest son and they had become very close. Fredric treated him more as a son then a grandchild. But Lloyd had grown up so quickly. He'd lied about his age, joined the Navy and shipped off to fight in defense of world democracy before he was fifteen.

Fredric just did not feel like a grandfather, hell he still had the fire down below. He tried to quench it by telling himself that he was getting older but the drive would not go away. He was a man of substance when he'd returned to San Francisco and had parlayed his holding by investing in the Homestead and other real estate development associations that were pushing the building spree and made him a wealthy man.

But this enterprise did not satisfy or bring peace of mind to him. The only peace he seemed to find was in the Japanese Garden and it was here that he decided to return to the sea. He commissioned a double mast schooner to be built in the Dog Town shipyard and name her "Effie". For the next few years he and his two man crew sailed the coastal routes up and down the Pacific coast hauling mining and lumbering equipment.

Bad News

Bad news seems to come in waves, in 1918 it came in the form of a telegram from the War Department that Lloyd's ship, the Jacob Jones, a Tucker Class Destroyer, was torpedoed and sank near the Scilly Island southwest of England. The Navy had picked up all the survivors but Lloyd was not among them and he was listed as lost at sea. Then what seemed like some good news, Lloyd had been found alive but was not expected to recover from his injuries and extreme exposure. He'd spent a week floating about on a raft made from scraps of wood and debris from the sunken Destroyer. He was eventually found by a fishing boat out of St. Agnes Island. Then in 1918 more bad news, Congress passed the 18th Amendment to the Constitution, prohibiting the manufacture, transportation, and sale of alcoholic beverages and the Tavern would have to be shut down.

1918 was a bad year for the family; they lost their means of a livelihood and possibly their son but as it turned out Lloyd was not about to give in and made a slow but steady recovery from his injuries. He had been in a great deal of pain and the English physician prescribed a new pain drug. The drug was originally synthesized by an English chemist, Albert Wright, in the 1870s and introduced a few years later as a pain reliever by the

Bayer Company as a non- addictive morphine substitute under the brand name of Heroin.

Riding the White Horse

Lloyd was never one for words but as he began to recover he wrote a letter from the hospital, St Mary near London. He joked about how it was the Germans who sank this ship and also developed a wonderful drug, a second derivative of Opium that relieved the pain and made him feel so good. But his Mom was concerned; to her anything made from opium was dangerous. And she was right, by the time the Navy discharged Lloyd he was totally addicted to the stuff. He tried to fight it, time and time again to no avail, and despite the best effort of the family he drifted off in search of some place he could hide and serve his new master, Heroin. They lost track of him for a year or so and then received the telegram informing them that he died of an overdose in Saint Louis. He'd died in an alley in the red-light district near the Missouri River waterfront, where no one cared, no one cried.

Lloyd's Home Coming 1922

Albertina accompanied Paul to the train terminal at the foot of Townsend Street. They were going to meet Fredric and Lloyd returning from Saint Louis. Lloyd had become Fredric's favorite, perhaps because Lloyd was about the age of his daughter when he kissed her goodbye, all those years ago. It's one thing, as bad as it may be to lose a child, but another to leave and then near see her again. There was no closer, just an empty avoid that could not be filled. And so Fredric and Lloyd developed almost a father son relationship. In some way the family felt Fredric was partially responsible for how things turned out.

As Albertina and Paul waited for the train she began to think about how talented and handsome Lloyd had been. No one could figure out where he got the wavy curly light brown hair and those clear blue eyes that looked through you rather than at you but he was a handsome devil. He had been so gifted; always the first to be chosen for a team, always the first pick of the pretty girls and such a fine musician, he could surely play piano.

She wondered why the most talented of the children should die; it should have been her or Paul. Then she thought it was probably because he was so wild, so full of life, so determined to live life to the fullest, perhaps he'd used up his allotted time too quickly or perhaps he knew that his time was limited and that's why he started so young. He was only twelve when he started to play piano in the dance clubs in the Barberry Coast area.

Dad and Mom tried to keep him out of that life but Lloyd was as stubborn as they come, and he was bound and determined to live on the edge.

He quit school and all but moved out of the house by the time he was fourteen, only returning to say hi, probably to comfort mother, to let her know he was alright. Albertina remembered the feeling of loss when he told her he was going to join the Navy to help defeat William II. Mom blamed Grandfather Fredric for the Navy thing. He filled the boy with sea stories and such. She felt that any war, especially this one, was just power hungry old men expressing their power at that expense of foolish glory hungry young men.

Lloyd's Farewell

His Mom and Dad had taken it hard but not as hard as Granddad Fredric. He held the telegram for a long time in silence, tears dripping from this cheek on to it and finally said, lord not another, how many can I bear? The duty of retrieving Lloyd's body was delegated to Fredric. Monty and Maria could not bring themselves to retrieve their oldest son's remains. To Maria it was pure hell and she was sure this was her penitent for the death of Elgin, her first husband. For Monty, who was not superstitious by nature but had a weary feeling that this was payback for some of the Filipinos he'd killed all those years ago. He'd never thought about the women, wives, sisters, mothers of those men before, how they must have grieved when they had received the news of their children's death.

Fredric wanted to have Lloyd buried in the military cemetery at the Presidio. To have a fine horse pulled hearse transport him to the Presidio and have the wake in the chapel but Maria would have nothing to do with it. She felt that those glorified military ceremonies were mostly about justifying mistakes, kinda like adding more chocolate frosting to cover a badly baked cake. When Lloyd was younger he said that if something happened to him, he did not want to be buried in the ground but rather at sea so he could join Uncle Thomas. Maria knew he'd felt guilty about surviving while most of his mates died at sea. He often said he'd dreamed of being united with them. Maria decided that Granddad Fredric should take his remains and bury it at sea somewhere beyond the Gate. She did not want a stone marker to remind her that her son, Lloyd was dead but instead wanted to remember him alive, kind of like when he shipped out and she could think of him as her young son forever at sea.

Return to the Sea

It was one of those beautiful clear San Francisco late winter mornings, you could see for miles and feel that you could almost touch the Indian Princes, in her eternal sleep, laying atop Mt. Tamalpais, her hair flowing gracefully down the eastern slope and her breast and feet clearly visible on the north slope, just where the Indian God had dropped her eon ago. As Fredric sailed towards the gate he passed a large deep draft coal burning commercial steamer, the Orient Queen. She was belching black smoke and drove a large wake as she plowed her way into the bay. Behind her perhaps two knots, a smaller coastal steamer also belching black smoke trailed the Orient Queen, kind of like a dog on a leash following its master. He marveled at how things change in his lifetime.

Once the bay was filled with sailing ships, Barks, Clippers and Sloops. The whalers and sailors that manned them are now long gone and have been replaced by unionized merchant sailors. As Effie, his double masts schooner with a crew of two cut her way through the wakes and the black smoke trailing the steamers, Fredric's thoughts drifted back to that day in the hull of the La Ninfa so many years ago and the gift of life that his Uncle Thomas had given him. A feeling of remorse so heavy that it almost buckled his knees engulfed him. If only he could return the favor and trade places with Lloyd. After all he was old, had lived a full life and Lloyd was so young and had so much life ahead of him. He wished he could return the gift of life but that was the gods business, he was only a mortal and not much of one anyway. He knew at that moment that he could not return to San Francisco, he was a relic of the past, out of step with time and the only thing left for him was the sea.

After passing through the Gate he sailed south along the coast and picked up the western trade winds. Three days out, the sea settled, Effie heeled nicely as trade winds filled her sails. She cut through the water smoothly on a heading of southwest. This was the sea he'd learned to love. This was the sea he wanted to commit Lloyds to. He ordered the helmsman to hold her steady as he prepared Lloyd for the sea. He opened Lloyd's coffin and carefully wrapped his body in linen. He laid his body on a plank that he had placed on the lee side. He cried softly as he recited the Lord's Prayer in Latin "PATER foster...... Et ne nos inducas in tentationem, sed libera nos a malo. Amen." And then in English "God this man, your son, my grandson, was young but he'd spent his last few years in hell, now it's time to take his soul to your house".

Fredric had always felt a void regarding the death of his wife and daughters. He was not there to bid them goodbye, he never felt closure. He was thankful that he was here to send Lloyd off. He ordered his crew to leave-to which caused the sails to luff and Effie forward motion to a near stop. He raised the plank and Lloyd's body slipped in the sea.

He could feel the trade winds on his face, he could smell the sea and he could hear her calling to him. He'd heard sailors talk about it and remember their warning but it sounded like a mother calling her child home and so compelling. He understood that it was time and he knew that the crew was ready and willing.

They had talked about working the South Pacific trade routes and fantasized about the warm weather and warmer women. Like all true sailors they were sort of misfits and only really at peace when at sea, looking for and talking about their next port of call. He saluted Lloyd, ordered the helmsman to resume the south west heading and said "boys it'll be awhile before we see San Francisco again". Effie's sail filled with western trade wind, she heeled to the lee side and surged forward throwing spay as she cut through the swells on her way to a different world and new adventures. The crew cheered and turned to their tasks and Fredric began to sing an old mariner song to himself:

Then pledge we a full measure
To the friends we left to-day,
Whose kind wishes hover o'er us
On our watery way

Day 16 Gold Gate Park

I *t was one of those days, you knew it was going to rain but still the*
sun would break through the cloud cover and be really nice. The
air washed by recent rain is so fresh. Georgia had talked about
how her Grandmother would take her to the Tea Garden in Golden
Gate Park when she was a child. I haven't been there for years and
suggest we check it out. That morning we agreed to make the trip. We
were 100 yards or so from the entrance when it started raining, real
hard. I grabbed Georgia by the hand and headed for an overhang in the
Steinhart Aquarium building. There is something magic about finding
shelter in the rain, like a momentary reprieve from the rush of life,
raining out there and getting everything wet but you are dry and cozy.

Oh hell I thought, I am beyond the point of no return. I looked at her,
she looked at me and without further adieu we kissed. The rain stopped,
we cleared a spot on a bench in the Shakespeare Garden by the side
of the Aquarium building. I dried the spot as best I could and we sat
looking at trees and shrubs freshly washed, their leaves emerald green
and shiny. The pack of black birds, the ones with a bright red insignia
on their wings, in their waterproof down insulated attire sitting above
the Shakespeare bronze likeness were persistent in a taunting chirping.
I wondered, are they just laughing at this couple of foolish humans?
Well, what do they know anyway? They are just want- to-be crows. So,
I don't know why the birds were taunting us but then I thought, guess it
was meant to be and it's not bad.

She broke the silence "My Grandmother told me your dad died
when you were young".

"Ya, my mother and I moved from her home in Glen Park to live
above the Tavern when I was still a baby". I replied.

Chapter 20
Homestead Montana Territory 1884

St. Peter's Mission

The Siksika, known as the Blackfeet by the Europeans, had migrated northwest from the Great Lakes area to present day Montana in the early eighteenth century. The whole of the North American indigenous population was being driven westward as the result of the European invasion along the eastern seaboard.

The tribe commonly known as Blackfeet consisted of the Siksika, Kaniah and Piegan. They tended to be militant and with guns acquired through trade with European traders were able to dominate their local rivals, Nez Perce and Shoshone.

After the Louisiana Purchase of 1802, the land that became Northwest Montana Territory was claimed by Blackfeet, United States and Great Britain. The United States and Great Britain had resolved their conflicting claim by 1846. The Blackfeet never gave up their claim but by the late nineteenth century had to settle for a portion of it, a 1.5-million-acre reservation.

Until the discovery of gold at Gold Creek and Bannack in 1862 the only Europeans in the territory were hunters, trappers and brown robed Jesuits Missionaries, the soldiers of Christ. One of the missionaries, Father Nicholas Point preached to the Blackfeet at a site, 10 odd miles southwest of present-day Cascade in the winter of 1846. Over the next dozen years or so the site became St. Peter's Mission. By this time, the early 1860s the Blackfeet population had been decimated by wars, smallpox and measles. A few remaining souls took refuge where they could and some at the Mission, even though it was a hated White man's establishment.

January 1884 was unseasonably warm due to the schnook, the warm winds from the Pacific, that had set in a few days earlier. A group of seven women departed the Northern Pacific Train in Miles City, Montana Territory. Six were in black robe, Ursuline Sisters and one in eastern attire, a lay teacher. Sister Amadeus, a small somewhat attractive, even in her habit, a strong willed ambitious hard driving daughter of a Tennessee Judge in her forties, the new supervisor for the Native American Mission Schools in the Territory, was in charge of the group. Lavina Copperfield, a petite woman with classic English facial features, large nose, round gray blue eyes, dark, almost black hair in her twenties was a recent art school graduate. She had accompanied the group in route to her new job. She had answered the call and an ad in the New York City Catholic paper for a Teacher to teach art to Native Americans.

Joseph Goodrich 1849-1918

I t was January 1901; ten degrees below zero, snow drifts were fifteen feet high. Two boys sat close to the fire staring at nothing, saying nothing. There had been a break in the weather, the winds had died down. Their father was outside attending to the animals, a priest from the mission was with their mother. Their father, Joseph, had come to Montana in the 1870s. He was one of thirteen children, the fourth one, of an Irish Canadian family. His father, John, their grandfather, had left Cork County Ireland for Montreal Canada during the potato famine of 1842. In Ireland the family had run a dairy for an absentee prodigal landowner. They were fortunate though in that they had food and shelter. The landowner was a righteous man and when the tax levied by the crown became unbearable, he disbanded the dairy and offered to send the whole family to America. Only John and his older brother accepted the offer. Their mother blessed them and wished them well but said "from Irish dust you come and to Irish dust you should become, I'll be waiting here for you".

John started a dairy, married a catholic French/ Indian woman and began producing children. He never looked back and he eventually became Canadian dust. His brother drifted down to the States and was caught up in the Union Army. He was killed for the cause, to liberate part of Mexico's territory and make it U.S. territory, and become Mexican dust.

At fourteen Joseph, their father was well equipped to venture out on his own. He knew about livestock and hard work. He could handle oxen as well as horses and mules. He worked his way across the young American countryside as a teamster. He worked on the levees in Mississippi, hauled freight to Fort Benton in Montana and then homesteaded land along the old Mullin Trail. He acquired a thousand acres of grass land and built a business of selling horses and feed throughout western Montana.

Lavina Copperfield 1860-1901

Their mother, Lavina was from a wealthy North Carolina family. She converted to Catholicism, at the time the only thing worse was converting to Judaism or being a Yankee, no well bread southern gentleman would consider taking her as his wife, maybe one of the carpetbaggers might. And so after graduating from Brown University, she accepted a teaching job, teaching art, at St. Peter's Mission. The Mission was established to teach the Indians not to be Indians, to adopt European culture and Christianity. When she met Joseph, she was in her late twenties and in those days, considered an old maid. Although Joseph was quite a bit older, she willingly accepted a chance to be a wife and a mother. They took up housekeeping in an old Bird Tail Stage Stop, a log cabin that he used as his home. He added a lean-to addition that included a bedroom and a nursery.

The cabin had dirt floors, no internal plumbing, a fireplace for heat and an iron wood burning stove for cooking. This presented no problems for Joseph whose creed for life was simplicity but it was a hardship for Lavina, who had been accustomed to the finer things in life. There had been some wonderful times on the ranch. There is nothing more beautiful than Indian Summer in Montana or as peaceful as a picnic down by Deer Creek. Before the boys were born, she and Joseph spent many late afternoons there, dreaming of their futures. But there were also heart winching times. Small bands of Indians, Flatheads Joseph said, would from time to time stop by the ranch looking for handouts. She'd give them the inner from livestock Joseph had slaughtered. He would get quite mad and tell her that that was a damn foolish thing to do; that they might return and steel everything. She could not in good conscience stand by and watch them starve.

Those Indians had lost everything, their land, their way of life and now those proud people had to beg from the very people that stole it. She told Joseph that no matter what, she intended to help them whenever possible but she did not really believe that she could truly help them.

She gave birth to two children, boys, without any complications but became sick with childbirth fever shortly after giving birth to a girl. The little girl, Irene was not well from birth and began to deteriorate within a few days. She quit suckling and lay quietly in Lavina's arms as life faded from her tiny body. Although her mother was ravaged by fever and pain, she would not allow the baby out of her arms until it was safely in God's hands. Death was nothing new to her. She'd seen so many Indian succumb to the White man's fever, White man's rules and White man's religion. She was a fine christen woman who had sacrificed so much to serve god. But still she was not at peace with her effort and possibly a little disillusioned with her faith. She believed or hoped that time lived under these hardships and the loss of her baby would count as penitence and allow her to go straight to heaven and bypass purgatory and to be with her daughter again, who would surely be there.

A Goodbye Kiss
Richard John Goodrick 1896-1940

The priest, his words forming clouds of water vapor in the cold room, gave the baby her last rights and took her from her mother's arms. He then gave Lavina her last rights. When he had finished, she motioned to him to come closer, then in a failed voice told the priest to bring the boys to her. She wanted to say goodbye. The oldest, Jacob, refused to see his mother. He loved her so, how could he say goodbye?

Perhaps if he did not say goodbye, she would not die. Richard, always the obedient one, went to his mother's side. She had lost all her color and what little youth she'd had. She held his hand for a long moment, trying to stay off the departure. Then knowing she must before the last threads of life were gone, she pulled him close and kissed him. Richard was only five but he understood this was goodbye, he'd never see the light in her eyes again, never smell her sweet presence again, never feel her warmth again. He hesitated then returned her kiss. It seemed to him that for an instant her face filled with life and she was his beautiful mother once more.

Chapter 21
Another Generation

A New Start

Richard received the news a few weeks or so before the official word came down from regimental headquarters, he would be part of the Army's cost cutting efforts. The Army was mechanizing and no longer had a need for a horse cavalry less alone the large veterinarian core. He'd been in the Army almost two years ever since being called up by the Greater Great Falls Selective Service Department district board. One of the two boys would be exempt since someone would have to run the ranch.

Their Dad, Joseph had passed away that spring, one of the first victims of the Influenza epidemic of 1918. A neighbor boy, Tom Kelsey had been wounded, a leg wound, in the battle at St Mihiel and hospitalized in Rouen France, the epicenter of the epidemic. Tom returned home and was hospitalized in the Veterans hospital in Great Falls. Well no one knows for sure but anyway before long half of the area was coughing and some were dying. Since Jacob, the older brother, was the executor of the estate, Richard was drafted. But Richard would not see any overseas duty, instead after basic training he was assigned to the veterinary corps at the Presidio in San Francisco. He did not know it but he would never see this brother or Montana again.

Brother's Keeper

Richard received only one letter during his Army career. It was the summer of 1919 and it was from an attorney in Great Falls informing him that the estate was bankrupt and the entire asset including the ranch had been sold to pay off debts. What Richard knew but did not want to admit to himself was that Jacob had used the estate money and money borrowed, the ranch as collateral, from the Land Bank. Jacob used the money to buy land free and clear in his name. When all the money in the estate was exhausted, he declared bankruptcy allowing the Land Bank to foreclose on the ranch. And so once the son of one of Montana's wealthiest ranchers was now reduced to a glorified stable boy in the US Army. And worse still the Army was sending him packing; he was totally alone in this world.

The good news for Richard was that draft horses and freight wagons were being replaced by trucks and sold as surplus for a song, as the saying goes. Like the coffin fleet of the eighteen century, where obsolete commercial sailing ships could be bought for almost nothing, an entrepreneur could buy horses and wagons for almost nothing and start a business. The irony here is the shift to mechanization that forced Richard out of the Army and into his business also changed the fortunes of Jacob. Jacob could or would not adjust to the new business climate. As the demand for horse-related goods declined, so did the profit. The land value dropped and he could not recoup the capital invested. He was stubborn and clung to his misappropriated land hoping, wishfully thinking, that things would improve. He ended up living a poor pauper's life in a tarpaper hut in the middle of the land he'd bought with money stolen from his brother.

The Shack

Perhaps it was the rocky outcrops of red chert there or just plain gold fever that caused the false gold rush in the Rancho. It was the eighteen fifties and shares in gold mines were a hot commodity in the East. Some shifty individuals, whose names have been lost to time, claimed to have found gold in the hills of Rancho San Miguel. On the Eastern slope of the beautiful Glen Canyon, about three hundred yards from the Northern fork of the Islais Creek, on an old, well used path, the short cut from the Mission Lagoon to the Canyon used by the Ohlone for centuries. They, the shifty individuals, dug a shaft, salted it with a little Sierra gold, build a gold miner's shack and begin selling stock. The rush soon died out, the scoundrel absconded with the cash but the shack remained, the gold mine is only an indent in the hillside that is now marked by a big old Cemetery Cyprus.

Over the years the shack developed into a small ranch house, the last on Sussex Street. The shack, which later became the home of the Goodricks, was constructed long before the streets were paved or sewer and water services were available in the Miguel Hills. Part of the issue was that the existing street grid for the city would not work there and the area remained somewhat isolated due to lack of transportation. As a matter of fact, the section of Sussex Street, the last hundred yards or so, was never paved. If you get the chance, go to the intersection of Elk and Sussex Streets and check out the sidewalk next to the red brick house. You will see that the old city sidewalk actually makes a hard turn into their yard. Originally this sidewalk boarded Sussex Street as it made a 270 degree turn and became a steep rutted dirt road.

Making a Living

The Cow Hollow dairies found the Glen Canyon and the surrounding hills ideal for their operations and relocated there in the early 1900s. This in turn created an opportunity for Richard Goodrick to apply his livestock and teamster skill to making a living delivering supplies to the dairy and hauling milk back to the city. He purchased a good rig, two horse trolleys, a type of large buckboard, two sound Shires draft horses and necessary harness from the Union Pacific Coal Company and started the Goodrick Freight Company. As his business prospered he was able to save enough money to buy the shack and an acre of the surrounding property. Before long he sold his rig and bought a used 1918 Chevrolet one-ton chassis cowl with a four-cylinder 21 horsepower, 224 cubic inch engine.

While he was doing just fine in business, being a bachelor was getting old, after all he was in his thirties and had been longing for a mate for sometime. His business regularly took him to the North Beach area to deliver and pick up supplies and there was a nice young girl, the daughter of a saloon owner that he was sweet on. He was not sure but he thought that she too had eyes for him. And so one Sunday morning, dressed in his best suit, he just happened to attend the 8:00 o'clock mass at St. Paul cathedral on Green Street, the same church that Albertina generally attended. She invited him to breakfast back at her family's home, above a saloon. The Saloon which had been closed due to the probation had been incorporated into their home and used for family functions. Well they hit it off fine, fell in love, were married in the church, moved to the shack, which was only temporary, the plan was to move to a real house and start a family but you know about the best laid plans. The stock market crashed, the depression hit Richard's business and the Goodricks had to make due with what they had.

Day 17 Bemjamond

I *guess it was just an old habit, back in the day one of my chores was to inventory the liquor in the morning and make a to-buy list for my uncle.*

So to past the time while I waited for the Travel Agent to call me regarding my trip to Costa Rica I began inventorying the liquor stock and just for the hell of it making a to-buy list. The process was interrupted by an aloud, urgent knocking on the locked front door. Although I was perturbed by it, after all the sign said "CLOSED UNTIL FURTHER NOTICE", I was also concerned by the urgency of the knocking.

It was Bemjamond Brovana looking determined and serious. " Can I help you"? I ask in my best business voice.

Without a hello he replied " I want a decision on the Las Arras, my buyer is getting impatient. It is urgent, do you want to sell the Las Arras"?

Just to piss him off, I said "you mean the fancy box and the thirteen coins"?

He did not seem to appreciate or see the humor in my reply and said" my buyers are important people and deserve a timely answer".

I have no idea where my next reply came from " I am just a saloon keeper and not that important but that fancy box was a gift to my GG

Grandmother. I do not know if it was a jest of love or just a cruel joke but be it what it may be, the Las Arras is now part of my family trust and that is where it will stay".

I did not know if Bemjamond Brovana was responding to a desire to purchase it or just plain jealousy about Georgia. It was clear our relationship was becoming more personal.

He took a long look at me and then said "I want an answer soon or the offer will be off the table".

I tried to fight off my response but to no avail. " Then here's my answer. It is not for sale".

He did not say anything, just turned and walked away. I closed the door and went back to my inventory chore.

As I sat behind the bar I scolded myself, you damn fool, that was part of my escape money, are you trying to screw it up?

Angry at and maybe feeling sorry for myself I poured a stiff drink of Jamison Irish whiskey and started listening to an old tape. Earth Angel Earth Angel I am just a fool, a fool in love with you. was playing, a song by the Penguins and I began to think about Hospital Curve.

That's a bend in the freeway 101 as it diverts around San Francisco Hospital. To build this curve in the freeway, a slice of Portola Hill had to be removed. So Portola Hill now has ugly scar with portions of the serpentine underpinning exposed. But I rarely think about that blemish as I drive through the curve, instead, I visualize the beautiful girls at Mission High School that lived there. They were mostly of Latin descent with long dark hair, olive complexion and gorgeous brown eyes. I only knew them from afar but thought one day I'd meet them.

In my mind's eye I see them as they were 30 odd years ago. Then I realize that if I met them today, they would be mature women with a lifetime behind them. A lifetime with some success, some missed opportunities, some wear and tear and of course some nagging health issues. But I do not care, for it's not that I'm impervious to the wrath of time and I'm sure my scars are clearly visible, It's just that I prefer to see them in full bloom as they were in high school, forever young.

Georgia I'm just a fool, a fool in love with you. I could feel my escape plan fading away and I could not help it.

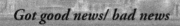
Got good news/ bad news

Chapter 22
New Deal 1932

Changing the Guard

FDR and the New Deal arrived, Federal Emergency Relief Administration (FERA) money began flowing into the city, public projects under the Civil Works Administration (CWA) sprung up everywhere and Amendment 21 repealed Prohibition. The Tavern reopened and Richard started working part time for his Father in-law. The Goodricks were looking for a new home closer to work when the good news came; Albertina was with child, the first grandchild for the Gregory's. But Monty had not lived to see the child, he surrendered to the old war wound last year. The chronic leg infection flamed up and he was bedridden for months before dying of Pneumonia at Letterman hospital in the Presidio. Per his wishes he was buried in the Spanish American War section, Presidio Cemetery. Maria, his widow, did not believe that she could recover from that loss.

They had been lovers, friends and partners in every respect but now she was expected to carry on despite losing half of what she was. She was still relatively young yet it seemed that her life was all but over. The Tavern was now her responsibility but she left the operation to Paul, her son and Richard, her son-in-law.

Clouds of War

Europe was at it again, Germany had launched a mighty war machine that was sweeping through the lowlands, America started to build up for the inevitable, and Richard got a defense job at the Naval Shipyard at Hunters Point. The defense job would exempt him from the draft and allow him to stay home with his wife and new son but I guess it was not in the cards. As he had grown up without a mother so his son would grow up without a father.

The USS CHICAGO, CA-29 was the second ship of five named USS CHICAGO. She was built at Mare Island Navy Yard in Vallejo and commissioned in 1931. She was the heavy cruiser, the first ship built to meet the Naval Treaty of 1922. A new welding process was used in order to eliminate excess weight and keep the cruiser within the tonnage limits of the Treaty. She displaced 9,300 tons and had nine 8 inch and four 5 inch radial-expansion mono- bloc cannons, six 21-inch surfaced torpedo tubes and two catapults amidships. She was fitted with two H Class Boilers, one for each fire room, that generated superheated steam that powered four turbines that transformed steam power into mechanical power that turned her six feet diameter brass propellers that could propelled her through the water at speeds in excess of 32 knots. She had a complement of 45 officers and 576 men.

The Ghost of Fechin O'Neil

In June of 1940, CA-29 was in the San Francisco shipyards for an overhaul. Along with the routine overhaul work, she needed to resolve a nagging problem with the black oil supply to her boilers, to be specific, the supply to number One Fire Room. It seems that under flank speed the boiler was not supplied enough oil to meet the steam demands. The problem was traced to a check valve at the feeder pump's input. For some yet unknown reason the flow of oil was reduced during flank speed maneuvers. The men of Number One Fire Room believed that it was the ghost of the young Irish Engineering Officer, Fechin O'Neil that was killed in that collision with that Tanker, SS SILVER PALM back in 33. He'd just left the Number One Fire Room and was returning to his stateroom when the Tanker plowed into the port side killing him and two other officers.

The men of Number One Fire Room said that, when the boiler was shut down (cold iron) during prolonged docking you could hear Fechin walking about the cat walks, especially near the fuel pump. After all, the problem first showed up after his death. The sailors of Fire Room Number One were especially nervous about the ghost stuff when the ship was in San Francisco, because that was Fechin's hometown.

On July 10th 1940 there was a small explosion at the Yard. It hardly made the papers with all the war news. A Naval Officer hand delivered the message to Albertina. The details of the accident were on the back page of the evening Call Bulletin newspaper. "A fuel line on the Cruiser, USS CHICAGO exploded while being repaired killing two workers". The line was supposed to be safe to work on since, the oil had been drained and besides black oil is not that volatile but when Richard used a cutting torch to free the check valve, the line blew killing him and another young man. Naval investigators later determined that the cause of the reduced oil flow and also the explosion was an uninsulated steam return line to close to the fuel line. The line had been rerouted during repairs for damage caused by the 1933 collision. It would heat up the fuel in the line causing the black oil to vaporize and reducing the flow.

But the sailors, especially the crew of the Number One Fire Room still believed that it was the dead officer, Fechin behind the whole thing. Scuttlebutt had it that the ship was cursed and many of her sailors put in for transfers. But there was no time for this nonsense, the Navy had a war to fight and the CHICAGO did her share. On December 7th 1941 luckily she was with the Lexington CVA16 task force some 400 mile southwest of Midway Island and escaped the tragedy of Pearl Harbor. She went on to fight in the Battle of the Coral Sea and at Guadalcanal. On January 30th 1943, she was torpedoed during The Battle of Rennet Island and had to be abandoned but she would not lower her colors and sank still flying them. Most of the crew was rescued by destroyers USS Edwards, USS Waller and USS Sands. Among the survivors there were a few sailors from Number One Fire Room and they collectively agreed that now Fechin O'Neil would at last be at peace.

Albertina's Pilgrimage

Albertina was part of the new generation that did not believe in memorial stuff. She'd only visited Monty, her father's grave one time in three years and then only because her mother wanted her to. So when the Navy offered to have her husband's body cremated, she accepted and his remains were returned to her in a blue and white ceramic vessel, along with a nicely folded American Flag. The Navy said he'd died in the service of this country and he was entitled a plot in the Presidio but she felt that he should be buried next to his parents, especially his mother. Albertina would cry a little every time she'd remember the story about how his mother had kissed him goodbye as she was dying.

It was a long bus ride to Montana and she was not quite sure if she could find St. Peter's mission. She was not in a hurry, after all Richard belongs to eternity now and she to this world. She did not cry and showed little emotion when she received the notice of this death or when she received his remains. People thought that she was in denial but she felt it was a waste of time to show emotion and besides no one else could really help her through this. She first needed to take care of business at home, she sold the Shack on Sussex Street and she and the baby, Johnny moved in with her mother above the Tavern.

Grandma Maria was delighted to have them, especially the baby, it was a whole new lease on life, and she had a purpose now. And it was just as well, the baby needed a mother, since Richard's accident, Albertina could not bring herself to mothering him. It was as if she somehow connected the baby to the accident.

The Mission

Albertina wrote a letter to the Catholic diocese in Helena, Montana, the capital, regarding the St. Peter's Mission. Monsignor Ballinger replied saying that he had known the Goodrick family, that the Mission was no longer being used but if she'd come to Helena, he'd arrange transportation to the Mission. So in the spring of 42 with her mother caring for the baby, war raging on two fronts, gas and other non-essentials on ration, she boarded a Greyhound bus at the 1st and Mission

Street depot and headed for Helena. The bus headed out across the Bay Bridge, built just five years earlier, through Oakland and then eastbound on US 40.

She fell asleep while passing through a nondescript suburb separated by miles of farmland, there were so many and they all seemed to be the same.

There's nothing quite as forlorn as an empty bus depot at 4 A.M., especially in a storefront depot on the back road of a one horse town in the middle of Nevada desert. Albertina has a two hours lay-over at Wells Nevada where she needs to connect with a northbound Greyhound. Two hours can seem like an eternity when you have nothing to do, no one to talk to and so she was relieved to feel, to see the night give way to the day. There is stillness during this transition, even if you have never experienced it before, you instantly recognize it. It is as if the powers to be are presenting a gift and there is a thrill of excitement about the whole thing. The swing doors stained and abused by time that provided an entrance to the depot became active as small groups of passengers, mostly young women with children, carrying their belongings in old well used suitcases or cardboard boxes neatly taped closed, began to fill the small storefront depot. This gave Albertina some comfort, a feeling of not of be alone.

The sweet smell of sage began to fill the morning air and she, despite her best effort to fight it, drifted off to sleep. Then fear, fear that she'll miss her bus, began to almost suffocate her and she forced herself awake. She started looking around and wondering about the people and where they were going when she noticed a woman and a young boy, about six, walking hand in hand. There seemed to be something familiar about them but they were oddly dressed, in homemade old fashion clothes, something like she'd seen in an old silent movie. They walked directly towards her and stopped in front of her. The woman, a green hand netted shawl about her shoulders, spoke in serene, kindly voice "my son is with me now and we are happy but I'm fearful regarding my grandson. Albertina could not believe her ears; who was this woman? She must have mistaken her for another woman, but then? but how? No, this was no mistaken identity. Then the woman said "It was hard for me to leave my son but I had no choice, you have a choice. Richard had to grow up without a mother, do not let John grow up without a mother or a father.

Those ashes you carry are of no consequence, do what you wish but do not forget to love and protect my grandson". Without another word, they turned and walked out of the station, hand in hand. For the first time since Richard's death, Albertina began to cry, softly at first and then an uncontrolled sobbing. She was crying for herself, for her husband, for her son. An older woman standing near her noticed that she was crying and she inquired if there was anything she could do for her. Albertina replied "no but thanks", then Albertina dried her tears and said "I needed to catch the next bus to San Francisco".

Day 18 Opening up

I was pretty much camping out in the sleeping room above the saloon, my sea bag serving as a closet, the cold-water sink and small mirror as my bathroom facility. I was starting to be more concerned about my appearance, new clothes, haircuts and shaving regularly.

OK this is nonsense, I might as well open up the rest of the living area. But it had not been used for a while, since my Mother passed. So I reasoned I'll clean it up a little and move in until the deal closes. Well maybe my subconscious had bigger plans but I did not want to deal with that.

But there were so many memories , birthday parties, First Communion, Easter morning breakfasts associated with that area. It would be difficult to deal with them? I thought I'd just hire a local cleaning crew to clear out all the old stuff, do a real cleaning job, clean out those memories. Then I rationalize, Georgia is in the real estate business and she knows people can do that stuff. So she agreed but only if I would meet her there before the cleaning started and sort out the items to be discarded. Paul, my uncle's, kid toys were packed neatly in a wooden fruit box and stored in a closet as if he expected to return one day and retrieve them.

Chapter 23
Forbidden Fruit

Paul's Coming Out

It was 1939 and Paul was thirty-four when he moved in with Glen, his long term lover. He'd tried to conceal this sexual preference, even from himself for years. He rationalized it by thinking, hoping that it was temporary, a sickness that could be cured, a deviant, an urge that first surfaced years ago when he was an altar boy. A lot of boys were doing it, a new game, allowing Brother Michael to touch their tools. His first complete sexual encounter with Brother Michael occurred after Easter morning mass. Michael had playfully massaged it a few times, causing it to swell hard. Paul had to admit to himself that he enjoyed this new game. Not only the activity but also the idea of doing something naughty, something forbidden excited him. Maybe this was the forbidden fruit he'd learned about at catechism. Would he go to hell if he partakes of it? Paul had read enough history to know that sex between males was a common practice with the Romans and after all, this was the Roman Catholic religion. Paul was pretty sure he knew what was up when Bother Michael asked him to come to his chamber that day. He was excited but tried not to show it but Brother Michael could see the flush in Paul's face. Michael was quite young to be an ordained priest and attractive, even if Paul would not admit it to himself. Paul allowed Michael to massage his exposed penis. When he began kissing him, Paul felt the rush of the climax but also the loss of innocence.

Maintaining Cover

Perhaps if Paul had not had that experience, he could have been normal, fall in love with a girl, married and had children. But from that day on he was aware that he was more interested in the males than females. He was able to hide this problem for a while but sexuality is one of those things that will not go away, it will not be denied. When he was younger it was still fairly harmless and easy to have sexual liaisons with various young men. But as he grew older it was more difficult to find sexual partners and still maintain his cover. To make matters worse, he really did not want to work in the Tavern but he felt an obligation to his family. He wanted to be an artist or designer and be a part of the Art Deco movement sweeping the country. But his Italian mother had taught him that the family came first and his main duty was to help dad.

Dad was injured in the Spanish American, a wound in the leg that became infected and never quite healed. It was difficult for him to stand for long periods or move the heavy beer kegs. So through his twenties and into his thirties, he dutifully worked at the Tavern and maintained this cover. After his dad died he became the man of the house. He was going to be a "confirmed bachelor", a single man all his life. This was not unusual in his day or for that matter throughout history. Men like Michelangelo, Botticelli or his uncle, Alfonzo had been confirmed bachelor.

Uncle Alfonzo had been married for a few years but it was a bitter marriage. His ante would complain that he would spend all his time in a bar and then not even touch her when he got home. Well Uncle Alfonzo was not really a bachelor because they were married in Catholic Church and there was no divorcing, marriage was for life. But married or not, Uncle Alfonzo moved out and shared an   apartment with another man. It need not be said that he was an outcast and not invited to the family functions but ante Stella, "what saint" as mother would say, was always welcome.

His resolve to deny his sexuality was badly shaken with the death of his father in 1937, the realization of just how permanent death is, the fear that he might live his life alone not sharing his love with someone.

He considered choosing a woman, there were plenty of possibilities but in his heart he knew that he could not satisfy her and it would only result in two frustrated people living together in denial. He was quite sure that his mother knew about this problem because she had stopped nagging him regarding marriage and stopped pairing him up with eligible women. Besides, Albertina, his sister was married to an Irish man and you know they would have children, the grandchildren mom wanted so badly.

Then as fate would have it he met Glen. Glen was his cup of tea, educated, discreet, a recognized local artist. There was never any question that they were attracted to each other. They knew within a few words and eye contact about their sexuality. As time went by they grew close and arrived at a point of no return, they were going to live together come hell or high water. They would maintain the facade of two confirmed bachelors living in the same house for convenience.

Paul had adjusted well to his life with Glen; even working at the bar now seemed to agree with him. While he was sure the some people knew the true nature of their relationship, San Francisco still maintained a live let live attitude. Albertina, his sister, had a child, John whom, to his surprise, he really enjoyed. Once a week, usually Wednesday in the morning before the bar opened she'd leave him in Paul's care while she went shopping. Paul would bring out some of his boyhood toys, trucks, trains and planes, for his nephew to play with. John would run them up and down the bar making motor sounds. When John was old enough, 7 or 8, he showed him the handbag in the safe. Monty, Paul's father had moved the handbag there from the drawer where it had been stored for fifty odd years. This handbag that had belonged to his Great-grandmother. To Paul it was almost magical and he knew John would like it too. After all he was the heir apparent and should be introduced to his inheritance.

Paul's Sojourn

While Paul was comfortable with their life, Glen began to grow restless. He wanted to live their life in the open. With Paul concern for his family and the residual hostilities towards open homosexual in the city, he knew it would be impossible. And besides, he wanted to grow artistically and San Francisco was stifling his creative growth. He decided to move to Paris with or without Paul. To Paul this relationship had priority and so he decided to sell his half of the tavern to his sister, move to Paris and bid abjure to his family.

Paris, like many ancient cities, Rome, London and Lisbon to name a few, is located on a river some distance from the sea. This provided the Celtic traders, known as Parisii, some protection from sea born threats. They established a settlement there in about 200BC. When the Romans conquered the Gaul in 52 BC, they recognized the strategic value of the location and built a city, Lutetium there. Pressure from the Germanic tribe reduced Lutetium to not much more than an armed garrison and by the end of the Roman occupation it was once again known as Paris. Paris was the Frankish King, Clovis I's capital but when he divided his empire among his three sons, Paris became just another feudal strong hold. It reclaimed capital status under the Capetian Dynasty and remains a capital to this day.

But it was not the Paris Glen was looking for, the Paris of the Lost Generation, an art and literary center where the likes of Hemingway, Fitzgerald, Pound, Eliot and Stein who is credited with coining phrase, lost generation, had flourished. Instead the City that had been saved from the Germans invasion by France's Renault Taxi brigade in 1914 and then surrender to the Nazi's blitzkrieg in 1939 was now a city in a Post WW2 Boom. Suburbs were springing up everywhere, industrial complexes were encroaching and the soul of the artist colony had fled. There was one saving attribute; the city was quite liberal with a vibrant gay community. With Paul's money and Glen zest for luxury they lived well. Glen, perhaps because of the lack of artistic success or may be just plain lust, began having affairs with a number of men. While this was a source of grief to Paul, he sincerely believed that love would prevail and things would work out between them.

But then the Count, or whatever he was, began courting Glen. Paul did not believe that he was a real German Count, he spoke both English and French with a German inflection but he went out of his way to avoid other Germans. Be that as it may, he had lots of money and he wanted Glen as a trophy. Glen for his part thoroughly enjoyed the contest and gladly gave his favors to the highest bidder. At last, Paul was no match financially to the Count and Glen moved to Rome as part of the Count's entourage. Paul broke, both emotionally and financially, packed up and returned to San Francisco. He could not bear the humiliation of working at the Tavern again so he opted for a state job and moved to Sacramento. It was a low profile with steady pay and suited Paul needs. The count eventually dumped Glen and he too returned to San Francisco. He was able to locate Paul and true love prevailed.

Day 19 Reflection
Ode to Mike Mc Kerry

*M*ke was a fair-haired lad that never knew his father but loved his mother dearly.

White Port and Lemon Juice

From time to time an item catches my attention and it kind of transports me to another time and place. For example, an old house set back from the street breaking the continuous line created by the rest of the houses. Sometimes they are corded off from the street by a small fence in need of repair and a neglected but once loved garden. I have this feeling that if I broached its boundary, I could be transported back in time and possibly meet some long gone and mostly forgotten resident. In Cow Hollow there were a number of small houses that survived the 1906 earthquake and fire. Some of the guys I hung out with lived in those houses. I had some time to kill so I decided to take a drive and I thought about that area, I had not been there for years. I was driving down a street, Greenwich street when I saw an old man painting a fence.

The fence was rather small and fenced off a front porch from the street. The house itself was rather small and appeared to have been built long before the rest of the neighborhood. I knew this house from years past. One of my high school schoolmates lived there. A man was painting the fence to match the house, an awful creamy pink color. The man was slightly bent over as he walked slowly up and down the fence inspecting this handy work. It seemed to me that I'd seen many similar old men through my life but never actually knew one. But there was something familiar about this old man.

I stopped my car and took a long look at the man and without thinking, more like a reaction I said "Mike". Sure, enough he turned and looked at me. I recognized the face through the years. He said "yes" I said "how are you Mike, it's been a long time" As he heard my voice I could see the recognition sweep across his face. "I'm fine Johnny" he replied. He was my classmate from long ago. The house was his mother's. He told me his mother was 93 and he was taking care of her. I'd never been close to Mike but I always liked him. He was always honest and a straight shooter. During our school years a lot of guys would hang out at his house. His Dad had died and his mother worked days, so his house was always empty during the day hours. When we were teenagers, we'd buy White Port, mix with Lemon Juice and hangout at Mike's house. We'd drink the mixture and listen to the black radio stations on the AM radio. But some of the guys including Mike got involved in drugs. I quit hanging out with him and had not seen him in years. Mike had seen some tough times, did some hard time for his drug enterprising and looked 15 years older because of it. For an instant, the fog of time dispersed and in my mind's eye I could see Mike as a teenager, his blond hair hanging in his face, walking with his head slightly bent forward, asking "want to get some White Port and Lemon Juice and hang out at my place"?

He said " want to get together and have a few beers? I said "sure" but knew we wouldn't. That was in my past and I was planning my big break out not rekindling my past.

Day 20 First date

*F*eeling like a highs school kid asking the homecoming queen to the prom " want to spend the weekend in Carmel? I asked.

For a moment Georgia seemed to be taken back as if surprised by the request. For the first time in years I had that twinge of excitement, fear and pain mixture of anticipation. I had not asked a woman out on a date in years. She looked up and said " how about spending the weekend at the St. Francis Hotel on Union Square, I love it there this time of the year. We can take the Powell Street Cable Car. It stops right in front of the Hotel". "OK" I answered. I was past the point of no return now, I think I may be in love, I have a desire to be with his women, be dammed with paradise.

Chapter 24
The Box

Journey of a fancy box

A fancy silver inlaid wood box was commissioned by a rich Italian banking family, the Medici, as a thank you gift to a successful Jewish banking family sometime in the early fifteenth century. No one remembers the Jewish family name, perhaps by design because in that period it was a dangerous business, doing business with Jews. But if you wanted to do banking business throughout Europe it was a necessary risk.

The Medici family were not the only wealthy Italian family doing banking business in the Italian peninsula at the time, the Sforza were in business in the northern area. The Sforza family came into possession of the fancy box and in the late fifteenth century it was given to the Borgia family as part of a dowry for arranged married.

The marriage did not last, the Borgia family annulled the marriage once the Sforza family had lost power and were no longer needed. The fancy little box somehow end up in the church coffers. Sometimes the church's treasures were used for logistical purposes, in this case as bribery payment to cover up an unlawful activity of a powerful bishop. Eventually the fancy box ended up in the treasury of a successful German industrialist in the early Nineteenth Century. Now this god fearing, church going Protestant gentlemen included the fancy box as part of his illegitimate daughter's dowry when she willingly became a Catholic Nun.

Day 21 Decision time

" " *I*t's been a great weekend and I believe you know I really like you". I said. "I need to understand where you are coming from; know who's behind this offer to buy the Tavern and what your relationship with them?. "Also this Bemjamond Brovana guy, what's the deal"?*

She shifted a little nervously on the bar stool. The weekend together was over and we were in the Hotel bar having a morning Ramos Fizz. It was clear to me we might have something going but I wanted to clear the air, especially about the Las Arras and Bemjamond.

She reached over and held my hand and looking directly into my eyes she said, "I may be in love with you." I almost dropped my Ramos Fizz.

"I've known Bemjamond for a while, we attended Real Estate school together. We were an item for a while. We liked to come to the Saloon, have a few drinks and visit your mother. So one rainy night, there were just three of us, a real slow night, we started talking about how your family had run the Saloon for years.

Somehow the discussion got around to the thirteen coins. Benjamin asked if the coins were in a box and said that sounds like a LasArras and told the story about the poor Peruvina boy. Your mother got the box from the safe". "Benjamin said that the box was really old and had a Medici family mark in silver. He said it was probably part of an important dowry. He was interested in historical stuff and was always antique shopping. He quit Real Estate and opened a coin shop in the Mission. When I got that offer to buy your Tavern, I called him and told him he might have an opportunity to buy the box and coins".

"Honestly, She continued, "I cannot divulge who is making the offer for the Tavern but I understand they want to tear it down and replace it with an upscale Law Office". Our relationship is strictly Real

Estate business". Then she squeezed my hand slightly and said "I hope you don't sell the tavern, I love that old place and would miss it".

Day 22 Never-Never-Land

and think of his age!

cute

*B*eing raised with minimum supervision has its rewards but also some consequences. Being young and free, never having to do your homework, never being asked where you've been or having a bedtime is a freedom I'll never forget. The streets of the city after dark are magical, a little dangerous but mostly exciting. It wasn't that my mother did not love me, she just did not have any time for me. She was busy running the bar and socializing. My Grandmother did most of the raising and she was too old to be concerned with school stuff. There were other kids to run with, mostly kids with single or no parents. We were all known to the cops, they had our names written down in a little book and judged us to be the next generation of losers, the most likely to fail, future yardbirds. How could we blame them for in fact we were looser in training, just like the kids a few years older we'd be into drugs and petty crime soon.

I remember my wake up call as if it was yesterday. That night I was hanging around a liquor store on thirtieth and Mission when I ran into Bill and Rabbit. Rabbit was a hanger-on and I never really like him but Bill had been one of the toughest guys around and a real stand up type. It had been a few years since I'd last seen him and was glad that I ran into him. Well as we began to bull shit, I realized that they were both stoned.

Bill's eyes were dilated and glossy. His words were slurred and all he talked about was getting high and how they broke in to pay phones to buy drugs. This was not the Bill I remember, it was like someone else was occupying this body and I didn't like him much. And worst still, I could see what the future held for me.

Rabbit started trash-talking about something and Bill interrupted him, "want to get some booze and go by Henry's place"? He asked. I know this game, they were now in the business, pushing drugs to pay for their habit. They were building up a customer base, It goes something like this: get you a little loose on alcohol and marijuana and *then get you to just taste. It's claimed a taste, a little heroin orally, will give you a buzz, no rush and will not hook you. Once you get the rush, an overwhelming euphoric pleasure, your only goal is to get it again and so your life is centered around smack.*

I also understood the real deal, It's not the pusher that gets you hooked, it's the desire to get ever higher, and that's your deal, and the danger. Their goal is to get you hooked and then you are a customer but you make the decision. Ok, now that I know their game, all I needed was to add this shit to my growing list of problems.

Now I just wanted to get some distance between us. "man that sounds great but I got to meet my girl, see you later" and I walked away. I felt like running but I did not want to piss them off and besides I had no idea where to run. I was seventeen, an illiterate high school drop out with a big chip on my shoulder, a rebel without a clue. I have a reputation for being smart, that is intelligent, but to tell the truth I was not sure if that was just bull shit since I never really tested my intelligence. And beside, the guys I hung out with were on the short side with regard to intelligence. Maybe that's why I hung out with them. I liked playing the part of an underachiever, you did not have to worry about failing. But that would be a cup-out to dismiss them, those guys, my friend did not have any illusion of superiority, entitlements or some sort of destiny. You got just what you saw and I felt comfortable in their company. I could not stand the goody two shoes that were busy trying to be what others thought was appropriate. In my mind's eye, I could hang out with the "loser" at night and compete with the best when I felt like it. But I figured it was time to put up or shut up. So I looked around, so to speak, for a change in directions and like my Uncle Lloyd chose the Navy.

And the Navy turned out to be my cup of tea. Initially the navy was not sure they wanted his boy with a broken nose and a jailhouse stare but after some major attitude adjustment and a few years of practice, I found a nice niche in the fire room as a Boiler's mate. The job is one of the worst jobs in the Navy but the beauty is that as long as you take care of business and don't make waves you're pretty much invisible. It was kind of like being in a hot dirty Never-Never-Land; you did not really have to grow up. So the years past, the sexual revolutions of the sixties, the war protest of the seventies passed and the Vietnam debacle passed by as if they were dull plays staged for someone else. But that's not to say I missed out on life. I enjoyed those years, new ports, new women, new adventure and every little responsibility. If only it had been a Never-Never-Land but at last, I may not have grown up but I did grow older and one day found I was classified as surplus, out of step with the modern Navy, a Navy that no longer needed Boiler men. I was invited, forced out of my cocoon and into the real world. And so I did the only thing I knew, hang out in San Diego in places where the forgotten and the want-to-be congregate. Like my Great Uncle I had no intention of returning to San Francisco.

But then my Great Uncle was a real sailor, I was just a member of the black gang, a snipe. And then one day I received a letter from my mother that said her time was running out and would I come home.

And now just as my opportunity to return to a Never-Never- Land, make my big escape and proceed on my quest for freedom, this desire for Georgia was getting in the way. She's too young, too smart, too everything and I cannot get her out of my mind. I had the escape plan. Sell the Tavern, move to Costa Rica with warm beaches and no responsibility.

Day 23 Into the sunset

*G*eorgia called me in the morning. *"You know there's only two more days and the sale contract will be void. The buyers are serious about the 30 days and it will take a day to do the recording stuff so really I need your answer sometime today.*

Really, the buyer is committed to plan B, another property in the neighborhood. I can meet you today and discuss this"?

"OK what time"? I replied.

"I'll be there in a half an hour". She replied.

This was going to be tough, we had become intimate over the last few weeks but I was not sure if it was the lasting type, a love that would grow or just a passing infatuation, mine or her's. Hell this scenario did not fit into my version of Never-Never -Land. I will have to shed my cloak of invisibility and face the real world as the mortal man with all his vulnerabilities, anxiety, fear and pain. My plan had me riding off into the sunset, untouchable, fearless and so on.

She had her business face on but not the suit, instead she had that real nice summer dress with a Levy jacket, to ward off the San Francisco chill. She looked great and began with "this is a great opportunity for you, no string attached cash offer" but then her voice softened, she looked away for a moment and then looked into my eyes and said" damn it Johnny do not lose what we have, I feel we have something real and precious, a gift that doesn't just happen. I do not know what you are running from but it is time to stop. The Tavern for better or worse is your heritage, your legacy and I would like it to be our heritage. Now there it is, a plan better than yours".

Then without another word, she laid the sale offer on the table and with one last look turned and walked out the door.

Day 24 Midnight

I laid on the old cot in the sleeping room above the bar for a long time, or it seemed like a long time but sleep would not arrive and relieve me of the burden, to run or stay. All I had to do was sign the sale document and I could continue searching for Never Never Land but no! that heritage stuff plus Georgia , and Sarah would not leave me be.

I could feel the presence of another person in the room. I recognized her voice even though I had only heard it once, "my poor boy what a fix you are in" Sarah's voice was soft with compassion.

"I too had to choose between running after my man or staying with my son. I cannot undue, forget or be forgiven for my decision. I never got my man and lost a life with my son. You will not find Never Never Land and you will lose the woman that loves you. This is the last time I will visit you but do not fret, this Tavern has our presence, stay and you'll understand, do not let them tear it down, it holds a fulfilling life for you."

Printed in the USA
CPSIA information can be obtained
at www.ICGtesting.com
LVHW040952200923
758788LV00004B/30